Worth Fighting 4

Pray for Martin
A.K.A.
"The Worth Fighting 4 Poem"

I was just a little boy
Who wanted to have some fun
And get down to business
Without hateration from anyone
Then I opened my eyes
It was there I saw my destiny
I stopped and looked up to receive
All the greatness that would come
Of course there was sacrifice
And no time to play
But in the end it was all good
For he sought a better way
Some things are worth fighting for
To get what you want out of life
Some hits a man has to take
But he doesn't keep it buried on the inside
United we stood
For the right to be what we wanted
Even if that means becoming the prey
And always being the haunted
Soon the day will pass
When I don't catch any sleep
Because He has come at last
And I didn't miss a peep...

Author's Note:

Although I write about gang members in this book, I DO
NOT endorse one gang over the other. Nor do I promote violence
of any kind...unless there is a revolution that is worth fight for.

I encourage all parents and teachers to read this book with
your children.

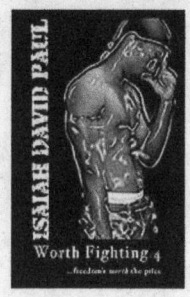
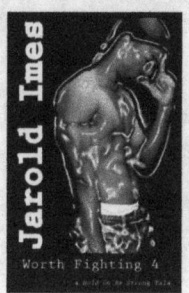

Classic Covers

Also by Isaiah David Paul

Worth Fighting 4

Isaiah David Paul

Abednego's Free

www.writesingwork.com

a literary entertainment company

Winston-Salem ■ Atlanta ■ Denver

Abedpego's Free & ᵂᴿᴵᵀᴱWrite Sing Work titles are published by
Write Sing Work, LLC, 6255 Towncenter Drive #1669, Clemmons, North Carolina
27012

Book Credits
Executive Producer: Jarold Imes
Cover Designer & Prompt Originator: Isaiah David Paul for Write Sing Work, LLC
Editors & Review Team: Shante "Glamour" Wright, Victor L. Martin, Melita Stinson,
CatXcan, Marcenia W. Waters & RoJay for MiddleChild Promotions and Bethany Hamilton
Freebird
Original Model & Photography: RoJay for MiddleChild Promotions

First Adult Trade by Vic Mar Publications, LLC January 2006
First Abednego's Free Trade Paperback Printing March 2007
First Write Sing Work Trade Paperback Printing March 2021

17 16 15 14 13 12 11 10 9 8

Worth Fighting 4

ISBN 13: 978-1-934195-84-0/ISBN 10: 1-934195-84-7 (print)
ISBN 13: 978-1-934195-71-0/ISBN 10: 1-934195-71-5 (eBook)

I was just a little boy...

A sea of pennies floated across the ugliest yellowish cream carpet on the floor. For a brief minute, I had a vision of caramel fudge bars stacked on a dinner plate right before my eyes. I stopped and inhaled the smell and for a minute, I thought I had smelled fresh chocolate coming out of the kitchen. The stale metal brought me to my reality and urged me to sit up on the floor. I looked at the pile of pennies I was counting in disappointment. The pile was as wide as a Monopoly board game and as high as the hardback Terry McMillan book I snuck out of my parent's room. I couldn't wait to exhale the nasty aroma that seemed to catch the back of my throat.

My father opened the door to my room and I looked up at him. He was a tall, cinnamon colored brotha with a touch of red sprinkles blended in. His hair was thin and the fine, coarse lines were in constant war with the Jherry curl he tried to hold onto. From a distant, he looked like a full blooded Apache, and if I had a dollar for every time he was mistaken for one, I wouldn't be counting these pennies now. Normally, when he walked into my room, he was beaming those Tic-Tac white teeth of his.

"What are you doing?" Dad inquired.

"I'm getting ready to open my own business." I answered without taking my eyes off the pennies.

"Oh really?" I caught my dad's interest.

My father sat down and pretty soon, he was counting pennies too. We had rows of pennies marching down the carpet away from the pile. They were stacked ten high and five wide. Each row had their own penny roll next to it and pretty soon, I was considering changing my plans to putting the pennies on top of each row, but I was afraid that the pennies would fall off. I knew I had caught my father's attention when I told him I was going to open my own business. My father sold M.Walker's hair products door to door. If anyone knew anything about selling products, it would be him.

"So what kind of business are you going to open?"

"I want to be a candy salesman." I answered proudly. "That school store they got at East is garbage. They don't have Airheards, Now and Laters, Mambas, none of the good stuff. And the prices for what they do have are too high. I figured if you or mommy took me to Sam's Club or some place like that, I could buy a big o' box of candy and sell them for a dime a piece and make some money. I should be able to double this in about a month."

My eleven, soon to be twelve-year-old mind knew what I wanted. I wanted to be rich and I was going to do anything and everything legal that I could get my still growing hands on, to get there.

"This is just a temporary gig until I can get something real going."

My father stopped counting and looked at me. I couldn't tell by the expression on his face whether or not he was going to approve of me being a salesman or not. I guess I couldn't blame him. All my life I had been talking about being a lawyer, putting all the bad guys in jail and helping the victims get back on their feet. Now all of a sudden, I was about making money.

"What you know about selling, Martin?"

"I know that if I got what people want, they are more than willing to part with their money." Wait a minute…that wasn't supposed to come out like that. I meant to tell him that people will spend money on products they want. I mean, that's what Daddy had been teaching me all this time about sales and all he talked about at the dinner table with Mom. Mom ran a beauty salon on Chambers and Mississippi and I swear it seemed like she lived there. Daddy would sell products out of the shop every now and then. Now here my parents were, working day and night so me and little Marcus, that's my four year old brother, could have everything a little kid could want. I'm talking like I'm going to scheme someone out their hard earn or should I say, hard begging for money.

"Part with their money? Just how did you plan on doing that? Sticking them in the back with a sharpened pencil?"

Shoot! This is definitely not going the way I wanted.

"No Daddy, I'm just going to show the products and if they like it, they buy. If they don't, I'll find out what they need and get you to take me to store to get it. It's all about customer service."

Whew! I think I saved myself from any embarrassment or extra explaining. I hope I did.

"So when were you going to hire me?" Dad asked me with a grin. I smiled back, "if you want me to go along with this plan of yours, you need to ask your mother first. I'll put in a few words for you but that's it. You need to know exactly what it is you are going to sell, how much it is going to cost, where you are going to store it, be able to take inventory, make sure that Marcus doesn't get his hands on your stash and handle the money books. That's a lot of work for you to do and go to school full time, which we still expect you to bring home A's & B's…you better not bring home a C or this little gig of yours is going to be over. And how are you going to invest your profits?"

"Malcolm! Martin! Where are you guys at? Marcus is writing all over the walls with a crayon. You know I don't got any money to fix this."

Ooops! Oh my! I didn't mean to get Daddy in trouble with Mommy! He got up and managed to avoid knocking over my stacked pennies. He gave me the look that suggested that I needed to get up and come with him. I really didn't want to talk to Mom about this now, I wanted to wait until after we had dinner and Dad could be at the table so I could discuss this with her. Damita Jo Little was all about business and I barely had enough room to piddle or peddle around the bush. I knew that the best time to get her to say yes would be after she had eaten her meal. I could hear my brother whining in the living room after I hear my mother giving him a few taps on the hand. The midnight blue Crayola crayon laid broken in two on the still ugly carpet, a bigger victim of Mommy's punishment than the culprit, who was crying as if someone stole something from him.

"I'm sorry honey," Dad gave Mom a kiss on the cheek, "I was in the room talking to Martin about a job that he wants to do while in school."

A job, I didn't say anything to Dad about no *job*. I'm talking about being in business for myself. Man, he just told! My eyes got bigger than I wanted them to, but I was trying to put on a front like what he said didn't even faze me.

"Well, you know you got to keep your eye on Marcus. He's a little sneaky and likes to get into stuff."

My father just nodded his head and I did the same. I'm so glad that I didn't get Daddy in trouble. Mom was taking off her work jacket as she was heading to the room. "Martin, what are all of these pennies doing on the floor? If you need money for school…never mind, just tell me after dinner."

Good. That was fine by me. I wanted Mom to enjoy her shower and get some rest in before I talked to her about opening my own business. I wanted this to come off so smooth that it felt like silk. Dad turned on the television in the living room and went to go talk to Mom about whatever it was he had to talk to her about.

"You guys watch Nickelodeon or something while I go talk to your mother. Martin, you make sure that Marcus doesn't write anything else on the wall."

"Yes sir."

I didn't want to watch television. I wanted to get back into my room so I could count my money because Mom and Dad didn't understand…I wanted to be in business and I wanted to be in business *now*. Not tomorrow, not next week, but right now. Before I could change the remote to one channel, Marcus had gotten up and ran in the direction of our room. I had forgotten the fact that he and I shared a room when I was stacking the pennies on the floor. *Man!* I know what he's about to do before he does and I quickly run into the room so that he doesn't do what I think he was going to do but I was too late. That little punk marched all over the room, kicking and stomping my money. I could feel my face turning red through my licorice colored skin and I think Marcus could see it too because he got scared and started to cry before I could even hit him. I punched him in the cheek anyway.

"Get out!" I tried to yell as quietly as I could so that I couldn't get in trouble. I didn't want Mom or Dad running out of their room ready to whoop our behinds because I decided that I wanted to open a can of butt whooping on my little brother. Little or not, he was wrong and should have known better about running through my stuff. I wanted to hit him again so bad, I wanted to cry but seeing him pout and get mad was even worse. I didn't know what that little boy was thinking but I knew that I had to try to keep my cool and keep my eyes on that little boy if I wanted Mom to agree to let me be a salesman.

The phone ringing temporarily took me away from my madness and I raced my brother to the phone, "Little residence."

"What's up chump! *Little residence,*" that was my best friend, Calvin, on the phone. He was always trying to do his imitation of me and trying to make me sound like a girl. I'll remember to get him for that when I see him at school tomorrow.

"I got your chump." I defended myself. "How did try-outs go?"

"They ain't lettin' no sixth-graders try out for the school basketball team. That sucks man." Calvin complained.

"Don't have a cow man."

"This ain't funny. I really want to play basketball this year! I've been dreaming about this since we were at Elkhart. It's bad enough we don't have a football team, but I got to sit out a whole year doing nothing."

"What about the Little Leagues?"

"Man, I want to play for the school. That's how Carlton getting all the girls and stuff."

Whereas I had the little brother problem, Calvin had the big and little brother problem. Carlton was in the eighth grade and one of the best basketball players on the team. He was the co-captain. He always had the flyest honeys trying to get at him--boy was he getting at them. He spent his time with them when he wasn't shooting hoops at recess. With his skills, he was running through girls like fresh spring water. Carlton would pick on Calvin and I when he thought he could get away with it when he was with his friends. I hated that tall, fake Denzel Washington, Johnny the Beanstalk— imitator with a passion because he always had it out for me. I didn't do anything only because he was my best friend's brother. Now on the other end, there was Casey. I swear that was the most annoying four-year-old if there ever was one. Always trying to be up under Calvin and I when we were trying to hang out with our friends. I never understood why Casey felt like he had to be around us all the time. Could have sworn he was a spy for his parents. I mean, Elkridge had plenty of four and five-year-olds for him to play with. All he had to do was pick one and get ghost.

"Them girls aren't even feeling Carlton like that...they just with him because they think he got some money with all them lies he be telling. Talking about he got a snake between his legs—I can't believe these dumb girls be fallin' for that line."

"Dawg, you the one telling the tall tales! Where's the man at that lives in the creek? I know he's not watching *Rap City* on that box television with the foil antenna on it."

"Oh man, I told that lie two years ago and y'all still on that?"

"Yeah man, but for real, I called to see if you got that math homework done. I didn't understand it and I need a little help. Smart *Alexed*."

I never understood why Calvin couldn't say smart aleck. The name was Smart Aleck, not Smart Alexed with a lisped the way he was saying it. Sounded just like our Mexican and Black friend Juan with that. *Alexed*. Juan was another story and I didn't have time to tell that one. Always mumbling something in Spanish...I hated that. That's why I made it a point to take Spanish so I could understand what he was saying. I didn't like being around people and not being able to understand what was going on. But for real, Juan Morales was mad cool.

Dad went to the kitchen to make dinner when he stopped to look at Marcus dancing to the song on BET. TLC was singing "What About Your Friends" and I wanted to know all about them. Marcus was off to the side, imitating the dance and trying to keep up with the dancers on tv.

"Daddy, I want some of them glasses. Can you get me some?"

My mouth dropped as I could hear Calvin laughing on the other end, "he's asking for Left-Eye's glasses, he probably don't know what's on them." Marcus kept doing the dance too, he looked so funny doing it but that's all good.

"If you don't turn from this fake Homey the Clown looking stuff on television...and Martin, get off the phone. Your mother is expecting a call in a few minutes."

"Calvin I got to go, I'll see you tomorrow. We're taking the RTD right?"

"Man, I don't want to get on there with them crazy people and them gangstas trying to scare everyone in the morning. I want to get to school in one piece. Besides, you know your dad is just going to drop you off like he been doing, why you fronting? I'll walk with my brother and the rest of those goons in the morning like I always do. Peace."

"Peace."

Mom came out of the living room and she was wearing a sweat outfit. It was just then that I noticed that Dad had changed into something different, too. I didn't care. Dad was almost finished with the spaghetti and the garlic bread he had just cooked. Mom took the salad out of the refrigerator and tossed it into a large bowl. That was her part of fixing dinner as she and my father alternated days in the kitchen. In no time, our meals were fixed and we were saying blessings at the table.

"So Marcus how was your day?" Mom asked as she was putting salad on her fork.

It was customary for our parents to ask us about our day first at the table, then Mom and Dad would talk about what they had to talk about. Marcus talked about the other kids at the daycare I used to attend when I was his age. Dad would share stories about walking all over Aurora, Colorado pushing M.Walker Products and my mom would talk about the people and the drama they were in when they came to her shop. The same ol' same ol'. Me, I tried to keep it different, whether I talked about some girl I thought was cute, my boys, the teachers or whatever. Today, I was ready to drop a plan on them. I wanted to let them know that I was the next generation of Little businessmen in the family and that I was ready to start now. I was kind of hoping that I could mention the business idea a little later but if I had to play my cards, I had to play my cards.

"I want to sell candy at school," the words just came out of me. I had a completely different approach on how I was going to lay this on Moms at the table but this would have to do. "The school store doesn't have anything and I think that I could make some money by giving kids what they want."

My mom looked at my dad and then she looked at me. I knew that she knew that was why my dad was on the floor trying to help me count them pennies. She smiled at my father and then asked me, "So what do the kids want?"

"Airheads, Mambos, Laffy Taffies, Warheads, Now and Laters, Jawbreakers. They want the good candy Mom, the *real* candy. My classmates don't want to wait until the weekend to go to the mall and scoop it up. They want some during the week, too. Plus, they don't want to pay sixty cent for a bag of M&M's and stuff when they could walk to Albertsons or Cub Foods and get that same bag for forty-five or fifty cents. Or wait until their moms and dads can take them to Safeway or King Soopers. There is a demand for this and I want to take advantage of it."

I can't believe I just used a big word like *demand*. I think I used it right. It doesn't matter I think I got my point across.

"Who's going to help you sell this candy? There are almost six hundred students at your school. What if your friends want to get the hook up, as you say it? Or, what if some bully wants to try to rob you and take your candy and your money? And how are you going to carry the candy and your books? Are you going to get in trouble for this?"

Mom was laying it thick like I knew she would. I was a little frustrated but I knew she was just trying to get me to think about what I wanted before I just jumped up and said this is what I wanted.

"Calvin already told me he would help me, and I'm pretty sure that Juan, Lester, The Twins and Franklin will help too."

"Franklin?" my mom questioned as she put down her fork, "isn't this the same Franklin you almost got suspended for fighting."

That was two years ago and Mom was *still* on that.

"Yeah, but if you don't want me to use Franklin, I won't. I figured he could fight them other knuckleheads if anything went down."

"Martin!" Dad scolded. Last week he'd gotten on to me about encouraging others to get in trouble and act a fool. My last comment made it appear that our conversation went in one ear and out the other.

"But with all of us selling candy and them putting in to get their share of candy, we should do alright. We'll be together when we sell it so we should be able to outnumber anybody that tries something with us. Besides, we all can fight."

My mom shook her head and she smiled. She knew I could fight and she also knew that Calvin could fight after all he had two brothers to practice on.

"I want to sell candy Mommy," Marcus jumped in the conversation.

"No Marcus, you're too young. I'll tell you what Martin, I'll take you to Sam's Club later on this week to see how much this candy is going to cost and we'll talk about it more there. I want you to see that money doesn't grow on trees because I'm only going to give you twenty dollars to get started and that's it. Your dad is going to help you set up a system so you can keep track of everything you have. Let me talk to some of the other parents and if everything goes well, you can start on Monday. But you better not get in trouble selling this candy Martin and you can only have two B's...the minute you slip up, your candy selling days are over."

"Thanks Mom and Dad," a smile stretched from one end of the table to the other. I could see $1 bills and $5 bills floating on that ugly yellow cream carpet instead of pennies. I was going to be rich. Besides, the paper money smelled better than the coins.

Who wanted to have some fun…

"So what did your parents say about selling candy?" Darren asked me.

I had turned my CD player off so that I could talk to him. I was into the *What's the 411? Remix* by Mary J. Blige. I had to look up so high that I thought I was going to snap my neck. I thought I was tall being five foot four, but Darren was a sky scrapping six foot two, at least that's what he says. I believed him too because he got a huge head and his head seemed to be a foot long itself. I had forgotten about Darren when I was telling Mom and Dad about the candy sales. That was my look out person, in addition to having a thick crew. Darren was just as tall and just as big as the eighth graders, if not bigger. Yeah, he was older than us, being retained in the fifth grade, but hey, he's still our boy. Most of his former classmates don't even associate with him anymore since he didn't pass with them. They won't step to him though. Calvin, Juan and The Twins: Ray and Trey had come over to our locker.

"Yeah, so what did your parents think of the candy sales?" Calvin asked while giving us dap, "you didn't say nothing about that on the phone yesterday."

"That's because I didn't talk to them then," I told Calvin and I waited until Lester and Franklin came over to the locker so we could discuss it. They were on a different team of sixth graders than the rest of us so that would explain why they didn't meet up with us right away.

"Mom is taking me to Sam's Club to get some prices and then we start on Monday."

"Naw kid," Lester took off his backpack...or at least he was trying to. One of the sleeves had gotten caught on his black and red Michael Jordan jersey.

"Hold up man, before you tear up your jersey," Juan offered to help. He was from Chicago so he wasn't going to let the jersey get damaged. Juan unhooked the sleeve so that it wouldn't get any more damaged than what it was.

"Thanks Juan. My mom took me to Sam's yesterday and I wrote down the prices right here. Plus, I got us some Airheads so we can get started."

"Word?"

Lester was always trying to steal my thunder, but hey, it's money to be made. He took out a box of assorted Airheads and we divided it among the eight of us, leaving the extras with Lester since it was his pack.

"We can make this money at lunch time. Then we'll give it to Martin since his mom's going to take him to the store tomorrow. Then we'll have more candy to buy and sale on Monday when we officially open shop."

"Well let me go ahead and put in for some candy," Calvin took out a dollar, putting his money where his mouth was. All of the other boys reached in and pulled out a dollar as well. Franklin gave me his lunch ticket and frowned. I looked at the ticket for one lunch and I smiled. We all knew that Franklin's aunt was on welfare and that this was the best he could do.

"Look at it like this, pretty soon you'll be handing me dollar bills instead of trying to cash in your lunch tickets."

Franklin smiled and we all went out separate ways to class. I knew that if Franklin really wanted to, he could sell his lunch ticket to someone for a dollar. Usually, you had to buy a set of ten for twelve dollars. Lunch really cost a dollar and twenty five cents, but you saved fifty cents buying lunch tickets every two weeks. Some of the older kids figured out that if they just bought a dollar bill with them, then they could bum a ticket off of someone who didn't want the meal, but just wanted some snacks or something. I, myself was going to sale my lunch ticket because I knew that I wasn't going to be eating today. Like Lester said, there was money to be made today and we wanted to hit with the candy sales first.

***

"So what are we going to wear on Monday? You think we should try to dress alike?" Lester asked. I swear that boy looked like the light skinned version of one of the Teenage Mutant Ninja Turtles. "We all got black pants right?" All of us nodded our heads.

"Let's wear red," Ray suggested.

"Yeah, let's wear red. A lot of people don't wear red." Trey added.

"Are you crazy?" Juan almost screamed when we gave the stare to calm him down, "all these Crips we got around here will kill us if we start walking around in red."

"Man, they ain't going to do nothing to us," Calvin replied confidently as we started making our way to the vacant basketball court. We had sold all of the candy we were going to sell in the first five minutes of lunch, "besides, what they look like stepping to some little kids?"

"I don't think my aunt's going to let me wear red man," Darren admitted, "besides, I'm an easier target among you short dudes if something were to go down."

We all looked up at him. If he weren't on our side, we probably would have been tempted to smack him.

"Red is my favorite color after black," I spoke up, "I don't see nothing wrong with it."

"I wish one of those Crips *would* come up to me," Lester went off at the mouth, "I'd sit on them."

"That's if they don't shoot your fat ass first," Juan cracked on Lester, "man, I'm trying to make some money, not get shot at."

"They are not going to shoot at us," I spoke up, knowing good and well that the opposite was true, "we just some little kids just like Calvin said. And even if one of them crazies did hit one of us, the whole neighborhood would jump…"

"The whole neighborhood would stay in they house and watch us get beat. Then move away from the windows so they won't get shot at. Martin, I'm surprised that you would let something stupid like that come out of your mouth," Juan chastised me.

"It ain't stupid!" Calvin raised his voice. "You know what, forget the Crips man. They some punks anyway if they got drive by with some blue bandanas over their face and shoot somebody then drive off in a car. That's some punk stuff."

"Calvin," Lester tried to warn him but that was of no use. When Calvin ran off at the mouth, he was faster than Speedy Gonzales and there wasn't no catching him.

"I hate the Crips!"

No sooner than Calvin had made that proclamation, a group of older, eighth grade boys had surrounded us. The leader, Freddie, was a basketball player who looked like the more athletic version of Snoop Doggy Dogg stepped up to Calvin. Calvin looked at him and grilled. I like that in Calvin because Calvin's not a punk, but now was not the right time or place to be acting all bad. We all knew that Freddie was the leader of the Crips at East, and the fact that he played basketball with Carlton didn't seem to matter to him at the moment. Furthermore, Garfield, one of the leaders of the Crips in this area was his boy. Word on the street was that Garfield was supposed to be a ninth grader at Hinkley, but he dropped out to handle things for his crew. I was just glad that he wasn't around.

"What was that you say little boy?" Freddie looked down and shoved Calvin. Pretty soon, we were surrounded by a whole bunch of eighth graders, looking to get something started. It was eight of us and I could see where Darren was coming from because he knew, like we knew, we were no match for any eighth graders. Calvin stepped to him and I was scared because I have never fought anybody bigger than we were. I was not looking forward to getting beat up by a large group of eighth graders because Calvin couldn't keep his mouth shut.

"I said," Calvin got in his face. I looked at The Twins, who looked at Juan, whose face was getting redder by the minute. Lester looked like he was about to pee in his pants, and to tell the truth, that might be the best move that one of us makes in a situation like this. I don't know why Calvin thought we were the Power Rangers, but he was about to find out real quick that we weren't.

"Man, my arms are little too short for this," Juan stuttered, letting the older boys know that he meant no harm. He was shaking his head and you could feel the beads of sweat bounce of his strawberry face. I would mistake him for white if I didn't know better.

Darren was the quick thinker and he quickly put his right hand over Calvin's mouth and used his left arm to pull him back. Thank God Darren was one of our peeps or no telling where this would have gone, "he don't mean no harm. He just run off at the mouth at times…he didn't take his medicine this morning. Come on Freddie, leave him alone. You know the boy is hyper."

Freddie and his two boys, Tony and Cedric looked Darren right in the eye. I balled my fist ready to hit either one of them if they jumped on Darren. I knew this would mean a trip to the hospital but I was going to have his back.

"Man, forget you little rug munchers! I know the next time he say something about Crip it better be something nice."

As Freddie turned away, Calvin put his middle finger up. Lester jumped in front of Calvin so that they wouldn't see him. The bell rung and the crowd quickly dispersed so they could go to class. Some of the teachers were making their way to the middle of the group. We were about to go from getting our butts kicked to getting in trouble in sixty seconds.

"Everything alright?" Coach Spalding, our physical education teacher approached us. Darren let Calvin go, who was steaming mad at this point.

"Everything is cool," Darren spoke up for us, "Calvin is just a little mad that's all."

"Well Calvin, why don't you come with me for minute? Work off some of this anger."

Coach Spalding wrapped his arm around Calvin's shoulder and escorted him to the gym. Calvin grilled all of us when he turned around. I don't know why, we was trying to save him and us from getting beat up.

"So we're going to wear orange and green right?" Trey asked.

"Yeah, orange and green go together, we could do that." Ray responded.

Juan and Franklin shook their heads. Me personally, I didn't care. I really wanted to wear my red shirt but considering the circumstances that might not be the best idea right now.

"Orange and green is perfect," Franklin offered his opinion as we all went our separate way to class, "I'll bring some extra Hurricanes gear if some of y'all don't have anything."

"I think I'll look good in orange and green," Lester gained some of his confidence back.

***

School was getting out and we all met at Franklin's and Lester's lockers since they were the closest to home. I hadn't seen or heard from Calvin since lunch period and I was worried about him. I was hoping that he didn't get suspended or sent home because I knew that Calvin's mom would have told my mom at the shop that something went down and then I would have been grilled when I got home. We started walking home and walked right past Elkhart Elementary. I could have swore that we saw Freddie and his group on the other side of the school, but I ignored them, hoping they ignored us.

"Wait up man!" Calvin yelled. We turned around and seen him running to catch up with us.

"Sup Calvin, man you almost got us killed at lunch time," Juan was furious at our friend.

"You don't understand Juan…I hate Crips. I hate them! I hate them! I hate them! They the punks that killed Carla."

We walked in silence. Carla was the oldest of the four children that Calvin's parents had and the only girl. She had gotten killed being at the wrong park at the wrong time trying to hang out with her girls and look at some boys two years earlier. Calvin, Carlton and Casey are a little sensitive when it comes to anyone talking about Carla, and will fight you the minute "your sister" comes out of your lips. I never had a sister, much less an older sister, so I really didn't know what Calvin was going through. Calvin's just a hot head in general but anything pertaining to his sister just made him go off the chain.

"Man, I didn't know the Crips killed your sister," Franklin was a little sad.

"I didn't know either," Darren answered, "but Calvin, you can't go trying to fight all the Crips because they killed Carla. You don't even know which ones did it."

"I don't care," Calvin replied, "if one did it, all did it. I hate them bastards! I don't care if they step to me or not."

"That was a smart move y'all made back there," a voice from behind us said. We turned around to see this guy named Bernie and three other seventh graders approach us. "Y'all was about to get tore up for real."

"Leave him alone Bernie," Darren stood up to his cousin.

"Shut up, Darren. That was mad stupid what Calvin did and you standing in the middle of it like Shaquille O'Neal."

We kept walking, trying not to make the issue bigger than what it was. We followed Elkhart Street all the way down to 6th Avenue. Truthfully, we could have walked the extra block to 6th and Chambers and caught the stop light, but we wanted to run across the street. It's almost like the rite of passage, proving our manhood. 6th Avenue was one of the busiest streets in Aurora, as it is an intersection with I-225.

Going north on Chambers Road leads to the notorious Montebello neighborhood, where legend has it a significant number of shootings and gang activities take place. 6th and Chambers was the playground our parents never knew we had. The thrill was in crossing the street and trying not to get hit. Feeling the breeze of wind behind our backs let us know that it was a mission accomplished. The cars went way past the thirty-five or forty-five mile per hour speed limit. Call us stupid, but this was better than bungee jumping or some of the other crazy things that people did for excitement.

Once we made it across the street we saw Carlton trying to kiss up on this girl at the gate by the apartments. He always was trying to get with some girls. I think that was all that was on his mind...girls, girls, girls, girls, that he do adore. Juan and Franklin lived closer to the 6th Avenue side of the apartments. Calvin, Darren and I lived close to the Chambers side. Lester and the Twins lived in these next apartments down the street from Chambers. I never knew what the name of those apartments was, but it didn't matter because Lester and the Twins were always in Elkridge hanging out with us anyway.

"Calvin, let me talk to you for a minute," Carlton caught up to us. The girl he was kissing up on was walking toward where Juan and Franklin lived. When Carlton got close enough to Calvin, he smacked him on the back side of the head.

"Ouch," Calvin yelled dropping his backpack, "what was that for?"

"That's for trying to start a fight with the damn Crips man. You know I play basketball with Freddie, man, trying to get me killed protecting you," Carlton grabbed Calvin's arm and started walking him to the apartment, "I'm make sure you get home too. Tell your friends you'll see them later."

Calvin threw the peace sign and we walked to our apartments.

"Orange and green right?" Lester clarified once I got to my door.

"Yeah, orange and green. Maybe we can get some T-Shirts made at the mall once the business gets up."

"We can do that."

I walked up the stairs and my dad came to the door. He waved at my friends and then put his finger to his lips letting me know that Marcus was asleep.

And get down to business...

My dad took Calvin, Marcus and I to Sam's Club so we could get the supplies we would need to run this business. When my dad, Calvin and I finally got around to counting the pennies again, we counted fifty dollars and seventy three cents. That was plenty of money for us to get some candy plus have money to make change. My dad talked me into getting a ledger so I could keep track of the inventory coming in and the inventory going out. He also promised to show me how to fill out my taxes so I could be ahead of the game. When I got home, I called all of my boys so we could divide the candy and get ready for school.

Lester was the first to arrive with his backpack and he had bought some stuff, too. We moved everything into the living room so that we would have some room to strategize and plan. The Twins called and told me that they wouldn't be able to make it but they would be at my locker first thing in the morning. Juan and Franklin came in next. We hadn't heard from Darren and truthfully, I was a little worried. I hoped that the altercation didn't keep him from being part of the group. We tried to call him several times but we never got an answer. And believe it or not, I didn't tell my parents about what happened either. It was kind of unusual because I always told my parents everything, regardless whether or not it was good, bad or ugly. I didn't want them to worry about me and the more I thought about it, the more I wondered if Darren had said something to his aunt. His aunt was a little over-protective of him. Then I got to worrying about whether or not the other boys had said something to their parents. I whispered in Juan's and Lester's ear asking them if they said anything and both of them said no. I knew that Calvin didn't say anything because he wouldn't want to worry his parents about it. Juan asked Franklin, who said no loud enough for everyone to hear.

The first thing we did was count the different pieces of candy we had. Then we divided that number by the total amount spent. Then we took each different type of candy we had and divided it by the amount spent obtaining the candy. That was how we set the price for everything. For the most part, everything was a quarter, but we had a few dime candies as well. My dad helped me make a chart with everything on it so that I could keep track of what we had and what was sold. Once we were done, we finished packing our bags and we did our math homework. Then when everyone was getting ready to go, there was a knock on the door.

My mom went and opened the door and I could hear Darren's aunt talking as they came in. Darren was dressed in his Sunday clothes, but that didn't matter to me because I was just happy that he was able to show up. I gave him dap and asked him if he told his aunt about the incident and he shook his head no. At that moment, I felt secure. Darren grabbed his bag of candy and sat next to Lester to help him with his homework. I looked at my dad and smiled. I was nervous because tomorrow is going to be the big day that could either make or break me as a business owner. I felt like I had the world resting on my shoulder.

***

I was ironing my orange undershirt when the phone rang.

"Little residence," I picked up the phone.

"Sup Martin this is Juan."

"Sup Juan, you ready to make this money?"

"Yep. What are you wearing?"

"I got this orange undershirt and a green tank top. I couldn't find any Hurricanes or Miami Dolphins gear. I think Calvin or Franklin got my jersey that Darren's father gave us last year."

"Yeah, that's what I'm wearing. I forgot about Darren's father playing for both of the teams. I forget that's the reason he living with his aunt all the time."

"Well, when I see them fools, I'm going to have to remember to get my jersey back."

"Cool."

I hang up the phone so I can continue to iron my shirts. I had already ironed some black dickies last night but I was trying to look fly. I had my black Reebox only because I couldn't find my Converses. I was debating whether or not I was going to wear my black bandana, but I didn't want to start anything. I put on my gear and looked at myself in the full length mirror we had in the hallway. I looked like one of the extra's from TLC's "What About Your Friends" video, but I didn't care. I was rocking this outfit and couldn't nobody tell me otherwise. After I put the iron and ironing board up, I walked into the kitchen where I could smell my dad cooking eggs, potatoes and toast. I was little ticked because we didn't have any turkey bacon or some chicken he could cook, but I was good.

"Groove me…baby…tonight. Damn boy, what is that you got on? Don't tell me Homey the Clown is your fashion consultant?"

"Oh you got jokes."

"I'm your daddy, I'm supposed to have jokes. Besides, if that is what you want to wear, then go for it," he went back to cooking and continued with this singing, "it ain't over...the party's not over."

I see now that I'm going to have to record over that Guy tape he's always listening to. Them guys ain't better than Jodeci. I ate my breakfast and walked out of the house with both my school bag and my candy bag. I had already asked Dad if it was okay for me walk with the boys to school and he reluctantly said yes. He already knew about everybody running across 6th Avenue, but he figured that if we all ran together, I wouldn't get hit.

"Look at this," Carlton pointed out, "the New Jack Swing is in full effect. I thought that this was going out style."

Some of Carlton's friends were laughing with him. I don't know why when in five minutes they going to pay me for this candy I got. I caught Calvin with my Dolphin's jersey on. That's what I thought.

"Oh, my bust yo'," Calvin tried to hide a Snickers, I meant a snicker, "I got your jersey on. But it looks good on me, really. You should have seen me trying to match them to some black pants."

"Whatever Calvin, you ready to make this money?"

"I'm always ready."

"What y'all got in the bags?"

"Dime & quarter candy."

Carlton took Calvin's bag and inspected it, "they got the good stuff, too. Airheads, Mambas, Laffy Taffies, Warheads, Now and Laters, Jawbreakers, they looking to get paid. How much is this?"

"The Airheads and the Now and Laters are a dime, the rest are a quarter."

"Got any candy bars?" the girl that was kissing up on Carlton the other day asked.

"Why you gonna pay for a candy bar when I can give you mines for free?" Carlton responded. I knew what he was talking about and that was straight up nasty. Some of the guys in the crew were laughing and the girl power walked away from them, "I'm sorry. I'm sorry. I was just playing. Roni come back, damn."

Well, with Carlton and his candy bar out of the picture, we made our first sales of the day. His boys bought up everything in Calvin's bag and some of what I had in my bag. He and I were grinning because my plan was working. As we got closer to the school we could see Carlton and Roni hugging and kissing again. They could definitely use a room.

We saw some of the sixth grade girls running up to us with dollars in their hands.

"Calvin, Martin, Juan, I know y'all got some candy. All the eighth and seventh grades saying 'go to The Twins' and 'The Twins' ain't got nothing," Dana, the light skin, heavyset beauty complained.

"I know y'all didn't forget about us," Moesha cut in, "we in the same grade. I know you going to hook us up."

"Of course."

Dana, Moesha, Lisa, Angela, Pamela, Renee, all the girls from around the way were giving us quarters, dimes, nickels, pennies for our candy. Cash was ruling almost everything around us.

"When can we re-up on this candy?" Darren came to the locker, "I don't have anymore and some folks want some for lunch."

"Tomorrow."

"Aww, man. These fine girls promised me a kiss if I could get them some candy for lunch."

Lester and Franklin came to the lockers each of them still had a bag full of candy. The Twins came back with some more money for the candy they took out of my bag. I told Lester and Franklin to save their bags for lunch and after school. It was amazing how all the candy went by so quick.

"Yo, let me holla at y'all for a minute," this guy named Second came over to our lockers. Second Chance was a seventh grader who went to elementary school with us. He was retained in the second or third grade, but now he's in his right grade. He used to hang with us off and on through out elementary school. Him and Franklin couldn't get a long and always ended up fighting. Me personally, I don't have anything against Second, but I knew he wanted to talk about business and Franklin was already down with the team.

"Sup Second," Darren and Second gave each other dap. Second gripped everybody, even Franklin.

"I'm good, I'm good. I'm hanging out with Brenda, Bernie, Christian and Eric. Love said he was at basketball practice, but I'm not feeling that. I think he lying 'cause he wants to play basketball, but I don't think he practicing with the team."

"Can't be doing that, my brother is having tryouts with the cheerleaders," Calvin said nonchalantly.

"Well, I was wondering how I could get down with selling the candy with y'all...or if I could provide security or something because I like what y'all have going on here."

"We might need some security," I mentioned. Second was speaking my language. Why have our boys fighting when we could get someone else to do the fighting for us?

"Aight, that's a plan, I guess I'll be wearing orange and green tomorrow then so I can support y'all. Let me see if Brenda wants to help. She can handle all them rowdy girls we got going here."

Another point for Second, "That's what's up." I responded. I hadn't even thought about these bad ass chicks but they need to be handled, too.

Second went to the North Hall where all the seventh grade classes were held. We went to the East Hall where all of our classes where held. We saw Freddie, Cedric and Tony walking through with this guy named Garfield. Garfield was one of the most notorious Crips in Aurora. Legend has it he got shot twice this summer in Cali. Garfield was one of those brothers that had an aura about him. Everywhere he walked he commanded attention. These Negros were supposed to be in the South Hall, but were hanging out on our turf for some reason. Some of the Hispanic guys were in the hall watching us.

"So when are we going to get in on this little candy business you got going?" Freddie asked.

"Sixth graders only man," Juan scolded before I could say anything.

"Sixth graders?! You could get more money if you had some eighth graders and some seventh graders in this piece."

"We straight…" Calvin looked Freddie in the eye. I watched these two go toe to toe, hoping that nothing was going to jump off before we got to class.

"I hope you are," Freddie remarked a he and his boys walked out of the South Hall and toward their own hall.

Rico, Arnez, Cisco, Texas and Ra-Ra were chilling in the hall looking at us. I didn't have anything against them but some of my boys had beef with some of their boys. A lot of it had to do with the fact that they were Puerto Ricans and Columbians and we were the blacks. That was the race war at our school, unfortunately. We had white people that wanted to be black, white people who wanted to be Hispanic… nobody white claimed being white. They were always mixed with something.

"They been on this hall twenty minutes waiting on y'all to continue what went down last week," Arnez, the lightest, almost whitest one said as he stepped to our group.

"Yeah, I was about to punch Cedric in the lip, talking all that junk," Ra-Ra, the big guy who was about my height said, "I can't stand them eighth graders man. I be wanting to box one."

I wouldn't call Ra-Ra fat, bulky or hefty yeah but not fat.

"Forget them," Calvin called out.

"Yeah forget them," Lester co-signed, "let's go to class."

We went to our classes, but I knew that something was going to have to be worked out with us and the Hispanic boys. I had a feeling that we were going to need them just as much as they were going to need us.

Without hateration from anyone...

Lester and Franklin sold all of the candy they had within the first five minutes of lunch. That had to be the easiest hundred dollars we had ever made. The best part about it was that we didn't even have to work that hard.

We had our table in the café that we sat at and some of the Hispanic boys sat at our table, too. I really wasn't looking forward to them trying to get all close to us lately, but I tried not to pay it any mind. The girls were sitting at the table next to us and they were socializing with some of the Hispanic girls. It seemed like the girls got along a whole lot better than the guys did. But that was because they can nab and pick at us and talk a bunch of junk.

Calvin was playing with his food, I could tell he was bored but I could also tell that he had something on his mind. I'm surprised that my boys didn't splurge their candy sales on junk food and trying to impress these girls that go here. I was proud of them.

"So who's better?" Texas asked with a mouthful of food, I surprised I could understand what he was saying, "NWA or Cypress Hill?"

"NWA," all my boys said.

"Cypress Hill," all the Hispanic guys said.

"Janet Jackson or Selena," Texas asked.

"Janet Jackson," all my boys shouted.

"Selena," all the Hispanic boys shouted.

"You crazy, Janet can sing and dance. What can Selena do?" Darren challenged.

"Selena can sing and dance, too. Besides, Janet ain't nothing but a ho," Arnez responded.

"Why Janet got to be ho?" Calvin jumped up in Arnez face.

"I'm just saying," Arnez closed the space between him and Calvin, "Janet singing about 'Anytime, Anyplace'…I'm surprised she wasn't doing it with anyone."

"Hey, hey calm down," Rico and I were pulling our boys back. Arnez cut his eyes at me, but I let that slide because I wasn't trying to be in no fight.

"Why he always gotta bring race up!" Calvin asked. The girls were looking at us crazy because they had been hanging out and getting along and couldn't understand why we were having problems. "Tell that white boy to go ahead with all that."

"White?!" Arnez vented, "I'm Italian, I'm not white. I got a little color just like you do."

"Yeah, whatever," Calvin dismissed them.

"It ain't whatever," Rico defended, "that's like y'all calling us Mexicans all the time. Let me let you in on a little secret ese, I ain't no Mexican, I am Cuban."

"How did you get here then? Got to come from Mexico, that's the only country south of us," Calvin shot back. Some of my boys were nodding in agreement. I really didn't want things to go down this way because we just got done having some good candy sales and I didn't want anyone in my group to get suspended because of a misunderstanding.

"Oh, I get it… just because I speak Spanish, just a few shades lighter than you, and my hair ain't nappy like yours, I'm a Mexican?" Cisco asked.

"Basically, y'all come from Mexico. That's the only way to get here," Lester was heated, "y'all come here and tear up stuff. You starting to take all the jobs that our people used to have. Then every time you see us, you always speaking Spanish and then when I ask you what you said, you look at us and laugh, like we're stupid. Ain't even cute."

"Am I speaking Spanish?" Arnez asked.

"That's only because I said something. Any other time you would have said it in Spanish," Calvin remarked.

"So, I'm a *Mexican?!* And it's okay for you to call me a *Mexican*. But the minute I call you nigger, you jump up ready to fight, like you doing now, nigga," Arnez responded.

"I'm getting sick of yo' nigga, white boy," Calvin responded back and pushed Arnez into the table.

Arnez jumped up and pushed Calvin back and punched him in the face. Calvin punched Arnez in the nose. Rico and I were trying to break up the fight so no teachers could suspend anyone.

"Y'all need to calm down, y'all gonna get us all in trouble," Juan tried to stand in the middle of the ruckus.

"Man, forget y'all! Y'all lazy puntas ain't nobody, especially you Juan. Traitor!"

Calvin started to run after Arnez but Darren and Ray were holding him back. Juan turned around and looked at Calvin. The tears were falling from his eyes like water sliding off a window pain. He wiped his eyes and punched Calvin right in the lip. I was holding Juan back to prevent another fight from breaking loose.

"I can't believe y'all said all that stuff about Mexicans! If I wasn't your boy, y'all probably call me a wetback or something," Juan was still wiping his tears, "so I guess if it weren't for the fact that my mama's black, I wouldn't get to hang out with you guys."

I tried to calm Juan down and he shoved me away, "get off me man!" I backed up off of Juan and watched him walk away. This was not going the way I planned at all. The bell rang for class and I walked to where my electives were being held. I had gym with Coach Spalding and Lester was the only guy I was cool with in my gym class. Rico, Arnez, Ra-Ra and Texas were in the same gym class. Don't get me wrong, I wasn't scared about Lester and I being the only black guys in the class, but I wasn't in the mood for no junk. Coach Spalding let us pick the teams for dodge ball and as luck would have Lester and I would end up on the team with all the white guys and all of the Hispanic children ended up on the same team. I forgot about Angela and Renee being in the gym class, too.

"Renee, Juan is so fine...but he looks real ugly when he cries," Angela was telling her girl.

"I hope I never see Juan cry like that again," Renee responded, "that was foul how y'all let that go down Martin and Lester. Always trying to be hard!"

"Shut up Renee, you just as bad sitting there watching it go down like a spectator."

"We're playing dodge ball, not sharing community gossip. Now if you want to talk, you can when you get out of my class!" Coach Spalding yelled.

So we played dodge ball for thirty minutes. I almost got hit with the ball twice. Arnez threw the ball at Lester's face, causing his nose to bleed. I thought that was messed up because he ain't hit Calvin in the face and he didn't hit them other people in our team like that either. I was ticked off and ready to go fight a few of them Hispanic guys myself, but I wasn't trying to get jumped or start a war either. When class was over with, I went to the locker room to change into my regular school clothes. I thanked God that I brought some deodorant or else I wouldn't be so fresh or so clean.

"Aye man," Rico put his hand on my shoulder. I pushed it off and faced him, "why y'all always got to start some stuff with us? I mean, every year it's the blacks versus the Hispanics...every year."

"Don't even come at me like that man because y'all start stuff too. You're boy—"

"Arnez...he got a name man, Arnez," Rico interrupted me.

"Whatever, y'all always go after Calvin, and you know the boy likes to fight. I'm beginning to think that y'all pick on us just so y'all can start a fight."

"So I guess we are going to be like this every year?"

"I hope not, but if y'all don't start nothing, won't be nothing."

"Aight look, check this out. We're all sixth graders. We can't play on any of the sports teams, we can't join any of the clubs, can barely get into any of the social gatherings they have here. You don't see them seventh and eighth graders talking about blacks and Hispanics, at least not publicly. Why can't we be like that?"

"Do you want it like that?"

"It would be nice if we could be like that for one year. That's all I'm asking for Martin is one year. Besides, our girls get along and hang out with each other on a regular, why can't we?"

"True dat. We could do it."

He put his hand out for me to shake. I did the same.

***

"Yo, have y'all seen Juan?" Ray asked.

"Yeah, I haven't seen him since lunch period," Trey responded.

"He'll be alright," Calvin confidence came through in his tone, "I want to see him about this lip though."

"You always trying to fight somebody, you know that?" Bernie came from behind us, "I will be so glad when somebody kicks your ass one time."

"Why don't you do it?" Calvin bucked and looked Bernie up and down, sizing him up.

"I wasn't trying to go there with you. We need a boxing club or something because you are too hyper and too violent. Doesn't make any sense."

"Well, if people like *you* would just keep they mouth shut half the time, people like *me* wouldn't have to put they foot in your butt all the time," Calvin picked up his bag and walked with the group.

"Your mouth dawg."

"Your mouth man."

"Calvin, wait up," Juan came running, "I got to talk to you."

Calvin's bag dropped straight to the floor. Darren looked at me and I looked at him and shook his head.

"Get your boy," Christian instigated.

"Look man," Juan sounded remorseful, "I came to apologize about punching you in your lip. I was wrong."

"Does that mean I get to hit you back?" Calvin repeated.

"No...you was wrong for that remark you made about Mexican's earlier. You hurt my feelings. All of y'all did. I'm black, just as black as any of you. But I'm Mexican too and I shouldn't have to choose one over the other. It's not my fault that I'm both."

"You done?" Calvin asked.

"Yeah, I'm done."

"Do I get to hit you back? I got to walk around with this cut on my lip and I ain't going out like that."

"You can't hit me in my face."

Bernie and Christian were laughing.

"That ain't funny. What you mean I can't hit you in the face? You didn't have no problem hitting me in the face."

"That's because you a hot head."

"Whatever runt."

Juan turned around and before any of us could see it coming, Calvin punched him right in the jaw. Then Darren, Trey and Ray run in the middle of it. Juan looked like he was going to cry again.

"See, he crying. Always crying. And I didn't hit him in the lip like he hit me, that's why I aimed for his jaw." Calvin's agitation grew with every word he spoke.

"But did you have to hit him though?" Trey asked, "That was kind of messed up what y'all said at lunch."

"Like you weren't agreeing with me, shut up!"

Calvin walked up to Juan and tried to apologize but Juan pushed him away. Calvin tripped and fell on his back and everyone started laughing. Juan kept walking.

"Yo Juan, slow down man," Darren called after him, "we can't be fighting among ourselves man. We supposed to be boys."

"We are boys," Juan yelled back, "but I need for that fake Tyson to stay out of my face for the rest of the day!"

"Let him go," I commanded.

Calvin got up and stormed off, too. I stayed on him to make sure he didn't hit Juan or try to fight anyone else. Then I thought about what Rico asked me earlier about if we could go one year without the blacks and the Hispanics fighting among each other. I was beginning to wonder how long we could keep Calvin and Arnez from fighting each other or Calvin from fighting anyone period.

Then I opened my eyes...

My boys and I just got done selling our candy for the day when I walked into the café and caught this fly honey sitting on the table. She looked almost like Janet Jackson from *Poetic Justice* with braids and the way her white doo-rag was matching her white button up shirt and her black pants. I caught her looking at me as I started walking toward our table.

"She look good don't she?" Calvin nodded his head in her direction. I shook my head yes in response as I sat down and recited my blessing. I took a bite out the fries I was eating, "that's my cousin, Shanice."

"You serious?" I couldn't believe it. Slightly turned me off because I didn't want Calvin to think I saw him like that.

"Yeah, that's my cousin on my mom's side."

"Man."

"You can go with her. I'm not going to stop you from trying to go with her. But Shanice is stuck on herself because all of the guys tell her she's cute and stuff."

"Is that right?"

"Yeah man. Her head is as wide as the Grand Canyon. Personally, she ain't *all that* to me. And I'm not just saying that because she is my cousin either. But she do need to be a little more humble."

Shanice walked to our table and started talking to Pamela and Renee. Every time her head moved, her braids seemed to swim like paper flowing in the wind. What can I say, I believed in magic. She looked me in my eyes and smiled.

"Calvin, what's that monkey-looking boy looking at?"

I think my heart landed in my feet. I couldn't move. It was almost as if a mirror were lowered in front of me and I saw a reflection of a black monkey jumping, dancing and eating a banana like he were Donkey Kong. I can't believe she called me a monkey.

"Why he got to be a monkey?" Calvin looked at me, "he look like a little hurt dog. Don't you need a new puppy?"

"Shut up Calvin," I stuttered.

"I'm just playing Martin," Calvin tried to hide a grin.

"It's not nice to stare, Martin. It makes me feel insecure," Shanice said real slow, almost like she were purring.

"In-suh who?"

"Girl, come on and lets go outside," Pamela got her things, "I can't believe you just called that boy a monkey."

Renee whispered something in Shanice's ear and the girls started laughing. I made a note to myself to charge all them heifers double on candy come tomorrow. I mean, who did they think they were calling me a monkey? I don't look like no monkey. But that's what I get for being dark skinned. Every time somebody tries to hate on me, they always comparing me to some animal…usually I get called a baby chimp or a skinny ape. Wait, that's what a monkey is. Anyway, if its not one of those animals, then they are calling me tar baby or making jokes about not being able to see me at night or something. I hate that, I really do. Mama says that its just kids being mean to me and trying to pick, but I really hate that. My boys know I hate that the most too…but I guess we all got things we hate. Calvin don't like it when you talk about his sister; can't pick on Darren for being too tall and Juan for being short or being half black and half Mexican. Lester's mom and Franklin's sister were off limits. And The Twins... man, forget it, them boys just love to fight.

***

"Calvin!" Angela yelled as I was making my rounds with the candy. "Make Martin sell the candy to us. We promise not to call him Curious George ever again."

I wish Calvin *would* try to make me do anything. He ain't my daddy, and even if he were, I'm still not going to sell the candy to them just on principle. How you gonna call the guy that got all the candy names and expect to get what you want at the end of the day? Now normally, money is money and I'm supposed to overlook things like this, but I had to put my foot down on this one. These chicks and that damn Shanice girl I'm still infatuated with were passing notes about me back and forth all during class period. Then had the audacity to be making ape calls as I walked by to get some water from the fountain. Martin don't play that!

"Alright, alright...I'll sell you the candy bar for three dollars."

I gave in. A sale was a sale.

"Three dollars! Have you lost your mind?!" Renee yelled, getting in my face while Lisa was trying to grab at the box. Brenda came just in time to see the ruckus and started moving toward me.

"Yo Martin, what's the problem?!" Brenda yelled and the girls made a path for her to go through.

"Martin's tripping, that's the problem," Shanice said being loud and shaking her head in two circles, looking like one of the old school clown toys.

"Brenda, these girls been talking about me and calling me monkey all during class period and now they expect me to sell them some candy."

Brenda was laughing and she shook her head, "you called Martin a monkey to his face? That's a classic."

Wait a minute! Brenda was supposed to be on *my* side, not them girls'. But she a girl, too, so I don't know what I was expecting from her.

"Martin look, go ahead and sell the girl a candy bar for two dollars and fifty cents. You know you want that money… and you do have to pay me."

"Two dollars and fifty cents!" Renee yelled.

"Man, forget that monkey-looking hood rat," Shanice grabbed her bags and got ready to go to the store, "I'll just buy the candy from my cousin tomorrow. He won't charge us three dollars for a candy bar."

I didn't say nothing as the girls left and continued to call me names and make fun of me. Some of them ran after Calvin and Franklin to see if they had any candy. I stopped by Lester's locker on the way home. I had seen him put some of the candy from the box into his bag.

"Who's the candy for?" I asked.

"It's for my brother Sammie. I'm going to wait here a little while and pick him up from Elkhart."

"Sammie, I didn't know that you had a little brother, Lester. I got one of those too, except mine just turned four and probably won't be in kindergarten for another year."

"Sammie is cool, don't give me no problems. He's real quiet and smart, too. I heard he's got a high I. Q., they have him in all those gifted classes and stuff."

The pride in Lester's voice spoke of a father who was proud of his son. He reminded me of when my grandfather would speak of me to his friends.

"Mind if I tag along?"

"No problem, no problem."

Lester and I walked out of the school building. We could see Carlton trying to sweet talk some chick. Normally, I would have tried to hate on his game, but I wasn't in the mood for it now. The school bell rang for Elkhart and all the little kids were running out of the building like they had just stepped foot onto Elitches. I was able to pick Lester's little brother out instantly. The mulatto kid had big brown curls that looked like Shirley Temple's all over his head. He had on a light blue polo shirt with khaki pants and some brown Timbs. He ran to Lester as Lester bent down to pick him up.

"Weeeee!" Sammie yelled as Lester spun him all around in circles. Lester had me fooled. He could have been Sammie's daddy if he weren't a virgin and my age. They look a lot alike except Sammie's skinny and his father is white, I think. "You bring me some candy today? You didn't let me have some yesterday and you promised me you would save me some for today."

"Of course man, you know I'm looking out for you," Lester put Sammie down as Sammie tried to show him the picture he drew in class, "what kind of candy you want?"

"You got any chocolate?"

"Yeah I got some chocolate."

I took off my back pack and pulled out a Snickers bar and handed it to Sammie. I knew Lester didn't have any chocolate. I envied Lester because I wished that Marcus could be as adorable as Sammie was. Maybe Marcus was like that and I'm just not around the house or in daycare with him long enough to see that.

"What do you tell Martin?"

"Thank you Martin. Your name is Martin…like the guy on the television show. My name is Samuel, but people call me Sammie. My daddy's name is Sammie, have you seen him?"

"Samuel!" Lester yelled, shocked at the question.

I smiled…Sammie had some mischievousness in him, too. I guess he wasn't different from other little brothers after all. "No, I haven't seen your daddy."

"I haven't either. I thought I'd ask."

Lester grabbed Sammie's hand and I walked with them the short distance of their house. I never paid much attention but Lester only lived five houses down from the school. Not bad.

"Are we going to play football after you do your homework? Or can we play Super Mario Bros? Let's play Super Mario Bros."

"Cool," Lester took his keys out of his pocket and gave them to Sammie. Sammie ran to the house and unlocked the door. "Thanks for hanging out with me for a little longer. Now you see why I save some of the best candy for last."

"Yeah man, no problem. Save as much as you want."

I gave Lester a pound and I watched him walk to the house. I looked into my backpack to see what candy I had left so I could give a piece to my brother. It wouldn't hurt me to be nice to Marcus for one day. After deciding what piece I was going to give to Marcus, I made sure my bag was zipped and I walked the rest of the way home. And for a moment, I was happy to be a big brother.

It was there I saw my destiny...

I gave Marcus some of my candy when I got home. He said thank you and he smiled. My father was at home resting after going door to door all day. M.Walker's had introduced their new cosmetics line and my father was building customers as he was visiting with the beauty shops today. Getting everyone to change from Fashion Fair was going to be a challenge because up until recently, Fashion Fair was the largest African American company making cosmetics for people of color. My mom was gearing up for a hair show that was getting ready to take place in Chicago in two months. She was experimenting with some of her wild and crazy designs on some mannequins she had brought home last week. She was reluctant to try some of her designs on a customer's head.

I had finished my homework and I got my dad to help me with the books for my company. So far, I had made six hundred dollars after I paid all my expenses and I had at least two hundred dollars worth of candy now.

"But his hair is just a mess!" the woman shouted, "I don't know what to do with it sometimes. And then he always wants to go ripping and running with his hoodlum friends!"

"I do not. I make good grades in school!" the boy shouted back.

Smack, "don't talk back to me!"

Poor boy, he should have known better to be talking to his mom's like that.

"My boy should be coming home in a minute. Let me see if he's coming in," there goes my mom volunteering my services again. I hated being the entertainer for her guests. I am not a member of the Jackson 5 or New Edition, and I shouldn't be subjected to the dance and sing routines she always having Marcus and I doing.

"I'm home Mom," I called out only to get whatever it was she wanted me to do over with. I did not feel like entertaining but the sooner I do this, the sooner I can count my money and prepare to ask my father to take me to Sam's Club again for more candy.

"Martin, come here for a minute. I got someone I want you to meet."

And that's the other thing I hate, when she tries to pick my friends out for me. She still not fond of the idea of me hanging around Calvin or forgotten the fact that Franklin and I almost fought years ago. Sometimes, I want to tell my mother to get over it already. What was done was done and it was time to move on. Of course, if she knew that the words were forming in this brain of mine, I would get the same smack that the boy got from his mom. It's funny because in the summer time, I would hate having to go door-to-door with my father selling hair products because it would be hot and the bag would be heavy. Dad would forget that I'm only five foot four, maybe ninety one pounds and that I can't carry his fifty pound carrying case all day. This was one of those days were I wish I were lugging around that suitcase, just to get me out of this mess. I come to the kitchen where my mom was working on some designs for the hair show and I saw the older woman first. She was pretty, almost like she was someone's grandmother.

"This is the Martin I've been hearing so much about," the woman said. The pride in her voice lead me to believe that she wished I were her son. I reached out to shake her hand and she gave me a hug. "I wish Garfield was a well mannered as you."

My smile fell. I should have picked it up but I didn't. I looked around to see Garfield sitting in one of the chairs in the dinner table. He didn't look too happy to be here either. I couldn't believe that my mother would let him into my house without asking me first. And now, I didn't think of the woman as being so nice. I tried to fake smile at the woman who claimed the devil as her son.

"Martin, take Garfield to your room so you can play Super Mario Bros. or something."

"Can we go outside?" I asked in an effort not to let that punk in mine and Marcus's room, "Marcus has his toys all over the place and I don't want him to get mad if I move them."

"You don't care about Marcus getting mad any other time so you shouldn't care now. Boy, take him to your room and quit trying to show out before I get my belt."

I would rather her get the belt. Undress me to my underwear and straight beat me. Better yet, let Dad do it; the whoopings hurt more when he does it. This way I would get the full fling action of being drug all across the room. Anything but let that punk into my room.

"Martin has a good idea, let's go outside," Garfield made an effort to help me. I didn't need his help.

"No! Martin is going to let you play video games in his room. Besides, I don't have time trying to chase you down from running with those cripples."

Newsflash! Your son is a Crip! The leader of the Crips in this area! As Garfield stood up and followed me to my room, I looked back to see if he was strapped. I hope that Calvin doesn't come over or call because that would be the last thing I needed right now. And now he's going to know how much candy I have. I just got Marcus to quit stealing from my stash and now I got to show this punk where it's at. I walk into my room and I sit on my bed. I picked up the *Number the Stars* book by Lois Lowry that we have to read for our Social Studies and English classes. I was more interested in the Danish people hiding Jews in their house and the teenagers fighting the Germans than entertaining the black Adolf Hitler.

"So this is your crib?" Garfield asked, chuckling. I was already starting to have nightmares about this fool climbing into my window, dressed up in a tan Nazi uniform. If I die in my sleep it's going to be Mom's fault. She'll probably be the one crying the loudest at my funeral.

"You could say that."

"Look, the only reason I'm here is because your mom wants to take some photographs of my hair for some portfolio she is putting together or whatever. As soon as she takes these pictures I'm out of here. 'Sides, I rather be jacking cars or doing it to my girl anyway. Bet you don't know what doing it is."

"I do know what it is," I quickly replied as I kept my eyes in my book.

"Look you little punk," Garfield snatched the book from my hands. I jumped up and got in his face. Yeah, this was a good idea, let Garfield beat me up in my house so Mom won't invite him or his mother back into my home. Dad would co-sign on that. I looked at this lighter version of Treach and saw how naughty by nature he really was. I could see the little whiskers growing from his upper lip. Now I knew why they called him Garfield. "I like you…little punk got heart. That's what I look for when I look for new Crips."

"I don't want to be no damn Crip!" I said sternly.

"Watch your mouth boy!" he put his hand on my neck. I punched him in his stomach, hoping that if he was packing the gun would go off and blow his stuff off so he couldn't do it no more. "You lucky I don't kill you while your mother is in the next room doing my mother's hair. Let me tell you something else too; the only reason you are successful at this candy selling game is because *I* allow it. So be thankful you were able to grate a few ends off my cheese, feeling me?"

I shook my head yes.

"So I won't snatch up your little operation if you don't blow the cover on mine. And I'll let you and that little runt Calvin live if you continue to behave yourselves. You know, I might atone for killing his sister. She had some nice kitty cat, too."

My eyes got redder and my fist tightened at hearing him confess to killing Carla. For a minute, I wished I were Calvin, or at least had the courage to do what I knew he would do. He dropped his hand from my throat and I snuck another blow to his chest as my dad walked past the room.

"Y'all alright in here?" he asked. I just knew that he saw Garfield's hand at my throat.

"We cool Mr. Little."

Garfield walked out of my room and my father walked in. I picked up my book from the floor and started to read.

"Martin it's me you're talking to. Did you just punch him in the chest?"

"I hate him!" I answered real quick and low, hoping that he heard me.

"Look, you stay out of trouble with him because he looks like he might be a little dangerous. And when he leaves, I'll have a talk with your mother."

"Don't tell her I hit him, or that he tried to choke me."

"Naw, never that."

I gave my father a pound and he walked out of my room. Marcus came running in with a little airplane running all over the room. I walked over to the window to make sure it was locked tight. I gave him another sucker and I prayed that if something were ever to happen to me, he'd grow up to handle whoever did it.

"Martin, you got a call," my dad called from the living room. I walked out and picked up the phone. My mother was playing in Garfield's hair. I shook my head and answered it.

"Sup Marty Mar!" Calvin was hype over the phone. "You started talking to these girls about the fall dance."

"Naw man, I haven't even thought about it. I've been reading this book for class."

"Man, you done read that book a thousand times already. Put it down and have some fun."

"I will after I finish this chapter."

"You think you can help me with my math homework though? After we play some video games on your machine."

"When you coming over?"

"About an hour or so, after Carlton comes in from practice."

"Cool. See you later man."

"Peace."

I decided then not to tell Calvin that Garfield confessed to killing Carla. Not that I didn't want to tell him, but I wanted him to live for a little while before he went ballistic and got himself killed. I couldn't live with myself if I had something to do with something happening to him... especially now that Garfield knew where I lived and could pop up at anytime. I walked to my room and picked up my book and continued reading. Hopefully, I'll never have to number the stars.

I stopped and looked up to receive...

I never thought that white T-Shirts would ever come in style, but here I was looking at a sea of black book bags bouncing off of the T-Shirts with black pants resting comfortably on some Jordan's.

"Get your jawbreakers man! Get your jawbreakers!" I heard someone in the crowd yell. I looked around and they had a crew of people passing out candy and making money. I could see Freddie, Tony and Cedric on the side of the school just laughing at us. Arnez turned around while passing out some more candy and looked me in the eye.

"Sup Martin! We got this!"

There are two things in the world I hated: people who steal my ideas and claim it as their own and people who mess with my money. I'm no Scrooge, but come on selling candy to fellow students was *my* idea. And I should be the one profiting from it! I looked at the brown boys stealing my hustle and for a moment, I wish I had a baseball bat so I could knock every one of their heads in. But you know what? I'm not going to let this get me down. I took out my bag of candy and went right into the center of the crowd. I knew I had what the students wanted.

"You still got the same candy?" Texas motioned as he was exchanging candy for money. "That don't work no more ese, you got to come with some new stuff."

"I think I'll be alright."

I walked to the different students buying candy and tried to get them to buy what I had in the bag. Call me spoiled, but this was the first time I heard "no" or "I don't have any money" or "I'll catch you later." I knew this was backward because usually, everyone came looking for me and my crew and some would be bold enough to meet us off campus so that they could get their candy first. I felt someone grab my arm and pull me away. I was heated and about to swing on Darren, but I wouldn't go after my boy like that.

"Come on Martin, it's okay. We'll get them tomorrow," Darren had a tight grip on the bag of candy still in his hand.

"No tomorrow, I want mine now," I tried to go back to the crowd. My customers were leaving me and it didn't feel so good. I felt my temperature rising and my eyes watering. I was ready for a fight and I was going to punch everyone of those fake snot nosed brats.

"Let it go man," Juan and Trey were trying to push me away from the crowd. "Quit crying and just let it go. We'll get our money another day."

I just shook my head and stormed toward class. Calvin caught up to me trying to tell me about some soccer game that we were supposed to be playing against the seventh graders on next week. I wasn't feeling him or the game.

"Yo man, chill with the illing," Calvin attempted to encourage me, "we'll wage war with those imitators another day."

"Looks like somebody beat you and your crew to the goods today," I looked up and seen Bernie and Second walking toward us.

"Oh, y'all think this is funny. Those damn runts over there are stealing my customers selling that tacos and burritos crap!" I responded frustrated and still teething at the fact that I didn't get my money today.

"Why they got to be selling tacos and burritos?" Second asked.

"Sounds like you are hating on they hustle," Bernie interjected.

"Man, ain't nobody hating on nothing. They just need to get they own hustle and let us keep ours," Darren said as the rest of our crew agreed.

"Darren, I swear you sound like an idiot with that remark," Bernie replied, frustrated.

"I'm getting tired of you calling me stupid man. Just cause I'm in the sixth grade doesn't mean I won't whoop your butt!" Darren brushed up against Bernie. They were looking eye to eye and were chest to chest. They pushed each other and Second got in the middle of it.

"Yo, what y'all doing? Y'all supposed to be family," Second held Bernie back.

"He gets on my nerves with that dumb boy stuff!" Darren shouted.

"What's up fellas?"

We turned around to see Eric and DeVante coming in our direction. Eric was on the track and field team for the seventh graders. No one really saw too much of him except on the track and field, were he was breaking city records and trying to establish state records. Eric was a pretty boy too, always in the new Karl Kani or Mecca. Word around campus was that his parents are rich and Eric was spoiled to death. DeVante on the other hand was a broke as a roach trying to get food stamps.

"I see y'all had a little problem with your operations today," Garfield boasted as he came closer to us. Freddie, Cedric and Tony were right behind him, laughing.

"Today was an off day," Darren said.

"I see," Freddie reached for Darren's bag. Darren moved it out of the way and smacked his hand back. Freddie was about to cock his hand back and swing but Bernie jumped in front of him.

"Back off my cousin man...he don't know better," Bernie defended Darren before he took part of the hit from Freddie's swing. Garfield blocked it so Bernie wouldn't feel much of an impact.

"Make sure your cousin doesn't get in my way," Freddie eyed Bernie, then he turned to face me, "you keep your little hot heads under control, or I'll make sure that the Hispanics bankrupt your operation."

The Crips walked off and Bernie faced Darren, then shook his head. The seventh graders walked to class and so did we. So it was like that. After Rico got in my face about how the Blacks and Hispanics need to work together and get along. Those puntas go behind our backs, steal our ideas and side with a gang. I really see how those fools roll. But you know what, it's all good. When tomorrow gets here, I will get my revenge on them, just wait and see.

***

It took a miracle on 34th Street, but I was able to talk my parents into letting me go to soccer practice. Carlton volunteered to coach us on our game so we were running over particular plays we thought we might want to try.

"Where's Rico, Arnez and the rest of them Hispanic boys?" Lester asked, "they know how big this competition is and they don't show up! Can't trust them, I tell ya'! Can't trust them!"

"I don't know why we have to let them play?" Calvin offered, "we've been practicing and working hard to get ready for this game and they don't even show up. We're supposed to be on the same team, but I guess they won't be playing."

"Yeah that's messed up," Darren complained.

We were practicing with Calvin being the goalie, well, at least we were trying. Calvin was real good a blocking shots and kicking long distances. He was the perfect person for the job. Darren was good too, but we need him on the field so that we could run some more plays. Franklin and the Twins were good defensive players and Lester and Juan were good at scoring shots. My job was to help Lester and Juan score; I could go for the points if I thought I could get it.

"Can I play?" Sammie asked as he ran on the field. He and Casey were on the side of the field playing with cars and trucks.

"No little man," Lester bent down and told him, "you have to be a sixth grader or a seventh grader to play."

"Well can I be a sixth grader for a day?"

I cracked a smile. I was admiring the little boy. Calvin on the other hand was getting frustrated and wanted to continue playing.

"We'll play after the game," Lester responded.

"All of us?" Sammie asked with a grin as wide as one on a clown.

"All of us."

"I ain't playing sh…" Calvin started to respond but all of us looked at him. He grilled all of us back like we did something wrong.

After we played for a little while, our parents came to pick us up. Carlton called us into a huddle and we got to see our uniform. I was feeling the orange and black polo shirts that Carlton picked for us. I was even happier to know that the Hispanic boys paid for their stuff. I didn't understand why they would pay for their uniforms if they weren't going to be playing with us but oh well. We even got Sammie a little shirt, too. Sammie went running around the park with his shirt on. His mom went chasing after him. My father and brother were waiting on me in the car.

"How come I didn't get a shirt Martin?" Marcus asked.

"I didn't know you wanted one."

"Don't worry Marcus, I will get you a shirt," my Dad told him smiling at me. I didn't care about Marcus having a shirt; I just cared about winning the game.

All the greatness that would come...

Sammie was running around selling candy for us to his fellow elementary students. I could tell that the boy was going to grow up to be something big. He reminded me so much of my father as I was watching him sell those products. He had on a miniature version of our sports outfit so he could look like Lester. The rest of us were getting ready to play our soccer game against the seventh graders. The last time we played them we were in the fourth grade. I remember those days because we would play soccer every day. It didn't matter if we had a soccer ball or one of the dodge balls, we always played. If we didn't play soccer, we played kick ball. It didn't matter. We always were playing some kind of game against some people in another grade level. The competition was thick, too. We hated fifth graders until we became the fifth graders and when we became the fifth graders, we couldn't stand the fourth graders.

Coach Spalding set up the game so that the sixth graders felt like they could participate in some of the team sports being offered at the school. We didn't have a soccer team in middle school, but that was the only sport that everyone could agree that they would play. The only thing I didn't like about playing with all sixth graders was that we were supposed to let the Hispanic kids play with us. That wasn't good because we didn't get along like that and now we had to work together so we could win a game. I hadn't forgotten about Arnez throwing that dodge ball at Lester either, but I had to put that to the side and just let that go. We huddled in our team and Sammie was breaking in, talking about he wanted to play.

"Naw, man, you got to sell our candy for us," Lester told him, "I told you we'd give you half of whatever you sold."

"I wanted to be out here playing though…I don't care about no money."

"But don't you want another game for your SEGA?" Lester asked.

"Yeah."

"Okay, then you got to go out there and sell that candy," Lester told him.

"Yeah, you got to sell the candy for us," Juan jumped in.

Sammie sighed, "alright, but do I get to play later? You promised that we'd play later."

"Maybe me and you will play later on okay?" Lester smiled.

Sammie walked away from us and he went back into the crowds selling his candy. I could see Angela and Renee pinching him on his cheek and telling him how adorable he looked. Sammie smiled and tried to dodge them as they kept playing with his baby face.

"Martin!" I heard Calvin yell at me, "We need to get into this game. Bernie and Second have been talking junk all day."

"And I got five dollars on this game so we better not lose," Juan added.

"Alright, alright already…sorry," I replied.

We got back into our huddle and started making plans. I looked up and over at the seventh grade team. They looked so tall and huge. We looked like we were barely taller than the fourth graders who had come to watch us play. Coach Spalding blew his whistle for us to start the game. Just then

Freddie, Tony and Cedric had taken their seats on the seventh grade side of the field. Garfield took his seat on our side. To make matters worse, Arnez, Cisco and the rest of the Hispanic boys were coming on the field in our uniform. They ain't showed up to any practices, had no interest in trying to get the game together when we first pitched the idea to them. Now all of a sudden we were suppose to let them play.

"What the…?" Franklin almost let a curse word slip out.

"No!" Calvin yelled.

"Hold up," Juan walked toward the group, "what y'all doing?"

"We're sixth graders," Arnez stepped to Juan, "we can play, too."

"No you can't!" Calvin yelled, "Y'all haven't been playing soccer with us before. Y'all ain't came to no practices. You didn't sign up…"

"Yeah we did," Ra-Ra jumped in, "we signed up right after you did."

"Man," Franklin became frustrated, "half of y'all didn't go to Elkhart, y'all went to Laredo and y'all didn't play soccer with us."

"The seventh graders from Laredo get to play," Arnez point to some of the boys who we didn't recognize from Elkhart. Arnez pounded his chest, "we get play."

"There goes my money," Juan mumbled.

"Man," Calvin pouted.

"You got a problem man?" Arnez walked up to Calvin.

Calvin looks at Arnez, shakes his head and walks off the field. The rest of the team soon follows as we try to convince Calvin to come back and play.

"Aww… po' baby," Garfield taunted us from the field, "don't want play with los mexicanitos?"

"Forget you Garfield!" some of us reply. Calvin wanted to run and punch Garfield but we all held him back. No, we got to keep him from getting all us of shot at. Garfield grabbed at his crotch area and then made a fist pumping motion at Calvin. Calvin flipped him off and mouthed his expression. Coach Spalding blew the whistle. I swear, the game hadn't even started yet and already we were getting called on. Coach Spalding came into our little huddle and pulled Calvin off the field. I could see Carlton and Casey in the stands walking to where Calvin was. We wanted to walk over to where they were at in the stands but Coach was directing us to get back on the field. I looked over on our side of the stands and seen Garfield laughing uncontrollably. I was so livid because what was supposed to be a fun game for us was starting to turn into a nightmare.

Coach came back on the field and blew the whistle for us to start the game. We had to move Darren to goalie, which hurt us because Darren was a good all around player, but other than Calvin, he was the only one good at blocking shots. Second volunteered to sit out for the seventh graders and we were ready for play. The seventh graders won possession of the ball and they scored their first point against us in like ten seconds. I don't know if Darren was paying attention because his back was turned to the field. We quickly retaliated by helping Juan score our first point. This was not part of the plan because we wanted Darren to be making a lot of those points for us, especially because he was taller. I looked over to the sixth grade section of the stands and seen Shanice speaking to this dude I had never met before. What struck me odd about him was that he was wearing all red and that he was behind Garfield. I shook my head because I didn't think boy was going to make it to see the game end. We kept playing our game and the seventh graders scored three more points to our one. Before we knew it, half time crept up us. I don't remember if that was allowed in a real soccer game, but we took one anyway.

"Thisé isé mesoé séme boule," Juan vented..

"What?" I asked. I admit, I was never good at pig-Latin.

"Man, Coach Spalding can come from anywhere! I know you don't expect me to say what I really want to say. I'm mad because Calvin is out for the rest of the game. We are down 4-1 and I feel like all this practicing we did to get ready for this game was being wasted. And to make things worse, these damn Mexicans don't know the plays."

"Wait a minute holmes," Texas yelled, "you need to take a real good look in the mirror because I ain't the only Mexicano on the field or did you forget?"

"And I'm Italian, not Mexican, don't make me tell you again," Arnez warned.

"Shut up," Trey or Ray said.

"Look, us getting mad ain't gonna solve anything," Darren reasoned. "We need to work together if we are going to catch up to the seventh graders. I don't know if y'all know this or not, but we are getting our butts kicked on out here on this field."

"If y'all would quit pretending that this is a black kids game and throw some plays our way, we could win this game," Cisco offered.

"If y'all had came to practice instead of pulling that stunt y'all pulled then we would give y'all some plays," Franklin countered.

"If y'all had quit pretending that we weren't sixth graders or that y'all didn't know that we signed up for this game during class, then we all would be better off," Texas answered.

"You know what?" Lester took off his shirt and threw it on the ground. We looked at him like he was crazy, showing everyone his flabby chest, "we should just give this game to the seventh graders because lets face it; y'all don't like us, we don't like y'all and because we can't see past race for one minute, we'll never be able to work together."

"Lester, I speak for everyone when I say put your shirt back on," Arnez commanded. A few people nodded their head in agreement as they watched in horror as his body moved before he did. "And we can play and work together. Y'all need to communicate with us more. Y'all *never* include us in anything and y'all think y'all the only ones that got it going on."

"Man, I know y'all know not talking about communicating," Lester put his shirt on, "every time we try to speak to y'all about anything, y'all just run y'alls mouth in Spanish. You guys speak English just as well as we do, yet every time you got something to say, it's that Spanish stuff. Speak English!"

"I can speak Spanish when I want to," Texas came back.

"Look," Juan said. I remember the last time we got into this confrontation, Juan was pulled into the middle of it and I didn't want to see that happen again, "can we put our differences aside for at least the next half of this game so we can try to win this thing? I am not trying to lose this game on some black verses Hispanic mess. Besides, I'm trying to win five dollars, not give five dollars away."

We all look at each other and went back on the field. Honestly, it wasn't just about black verses Hispanic race relations. That was part of it but that was not a big deal. If I felt that I hated Hispanics, I wouldn't be friends with Juan. I know that he was half us, half them. I didn't like how they just assumed they could join in our little game. We eat lunch with these cats everyday and not one time did they mention to us, "Hey, we want to be in the game" or "when y'all practicing?" And I know they've heard us talking about the upcoming game because they heard us speak about it at lunch and talking mess to the seventh graders. At the same time, if the seventh graders got beef amongst each other, we don't know about it. That's how we need to play.

So we get out on the field and for the most part, things change a little. Texas scored two points for us back to back but we were still behind five to three. We started working together as a team as opposed to two individual units. I'm not gonna lie, we should have been doing that all along but we've never had to work together before, so we didn't see a need to start doing it now. In the end, we lost the game six to four.

"NowLaters! NowLaters!" Sammie yelled as the seventh graders were enjoying their victory. Some of the seventh grade girls were pulling out their dollar bills and buying candy from the boy. Yep, I was right, he reminds me of my father and somebody else I know. One day, he'll be on the cover of *Black Enterprise*, now or later.

Of course there was sacrifice...

Even though we lost the soccer game the other day, we weren't going to let that get us down. Over the intercom, the principal announced that the school was going to allow the sixth graders to attend this year's school social. Naturally, the seventh and the eighth graders were upset because they weren't allowed to go when they were sixth graders. Some of them openly questioned whether or not we could dance or hang with them on the dance floor.

Darren hooked up with this fine girl named Amerie. She was a seventh grader who hung out with Brenda. She had long, moreno colored hair, straight as spaghetti. Her skin was the nice mixture of coffee and cream. Those eyes man, damn, almond-shaped with chocolate Kisses inside. I ain't know they made girls *this fine*. She looked kinda like Salli Richardson in the *Posse* movie. She claimed that one of her grandparents was part of the Apache tribe, but she's from Mississippi. A southern girl...sassy and sophisticated. Juan also had a nice looking girl from the seventh grade, too. I don't remember her name, but I do know she had wild, nappy hair to be Cuban. Calvin swore he was going to get him some at the dance, but we all laughed him off. Ray and Trey said they weren't going to go; something about playing basketball at the YMCA. Franklin had finally asked Renee if she would go to the dance with him. I swear he's had a crush on that girl for the longest. After blushing a little bit, she finally said yeah.

Lester wasn't going to go because he was going to hang out with Sammie and some of Sammie's classmates at Skate City.

I should have hung out with him and Sammie and maybe brought Marcus along with us. But instead, I decided to try my luck with Shanice again. I loved her smile, but she wasn't diggin' me. She claimed the only reason she was going to meet me at the dance was because no one else would go with her and she got tired of me calling. Persistence paid off.

The cost of the dance was three dollars or we could donate six canned foods to the event. My boys and I pulled our money together and talked my father into taking us to Sam's Club to buy some canned goods. This way, we could pay less for the canned food and the dance. I know that sounds trifling but they were just going to go to Sam's Club with the money to get the food anyway. We were just saving them a trip.

We had decided that we were going to wear button up shirts with orange or green shirts under them. Calvin's father volunteered to take me and his sons to the dance. Carlton even let Calvin and I wear some his body spray. It was one of those knock off Jordan scents; but we were just happy to have some on. We felt like we were grown.

We got to the gym and Bell Biv DeVoe were asking the girls to "Do Me." Salt 'N' Pepa were encouraging girls to "Push It." I wish I were "A L'il Bit Taller." With all this going on, I'm surprised they weren't talking about sex.

"Look," Carlton putting his hands on Calvin and my shoulders, "I'm out here trying to get some honeys. Some, something—something, if you know what I mean. I can leave y'all two alone and you not get into trouble right?"

"Of course," Calvin tried to get Carlton's hand off his shoulder, "I'm trying to get some, something—something, myself."

"Boy you are a mess," Carlton laughed at him, "Martin, watch after Calvin and make sure he don't fight nobody or mess with nobody. I'm not trying to babysit."

"Carlton, chill, I'm not going to get into trouble." Calvin grilled Carlton and balled his fist like he was going to punch him. Then he smirked like he has something devious planned.

Carlton and I looked at each other. I could tell by the way that he said it that he was looking to get at somebody. I wasn't trying to be the babysitter either, but I needed for Calvin to stay out of trouble.

We *finally* got into the dance and we could hear SWV singing, "I'm So Into You." Carlton was grinning at this one girl who was smiling back and I knew he was going to get into her. I could see Shanice dancing on the floor and I wanted to be into her. I didn't know what I was going to do. She was dancing with some seventh grader. I waited until the song was over and she walked away from him before I approached her.

"Sup Shanice," I called her name. I was so nervous. I could feel the sweating dripping from my palms and my legs shaking.

"Hey Martin, I didn't know you were going to be here." She lied because I asked her about fifty-eleven times to go out with me.

I decided to play it off, "well, would you like to dance?"

Mary J. Blige was letting me know that she had "Real Love" when she told me, "I would love too, but I'm here with Allen."

The younger and fake version of DJ Quick came walking back with two cups. When he handed one to Shanice, I noticed the red bandana in the left side of his pants pocket. He was the kid I saw behind Garfield at the game.

So he did survive...what a miracle. I heard that him and Garfield got into it again and that he'd gotten shot. I knew he was rolling deep with the Bloods and those boys and the Crips were always fighting and shooting at one another.

"Sup l'il man," Allen gave me a pound. I wanted to leave him hanging but I returned his pound instead.

I watched as Allen palmed Shanice's behind as they walked by. I don't even know why I agreed to go to the dance. To make matters worse, "All I Do," by Troop was playing and I was going to be up against the wall, thinking about Shanice. I was starting to hate her smile as she and Allen were dancing so close, he could've picked her up and carried her. Al B. Sure said that she'd be "Off on Her Own" but didn't want to be cruel like Bobby Brown so I just left it as it was.

I was happier when TLC's "Hat 2 Da Back" came on. Allen pulled out his doo rag and put it on. Shanice had on a red cap and she placed hers at an angle to the back. A lot of people went from clean, presentable gear to wanna be gangstas. I looked for Calvin to make sure he wasn't into any trouble. I found him whispering into some l'il Mexican girl's ear. Juan, Darren and Franklin were having a good time with their dates. I found Carlton bumping and grinding with some girl. R. Kelly wouldn't have seen anything wrong with that. On the other hand I did, so I was about to leave the party. I wasn't having fun anyway.

As I was getting ready to leave, I went over to the drink area. I was debating whether or not I was going to get something to drink. I picked up a cup and I saw Freddie and some chick kissing against the wall. I dropped my cup and headed to the door. I had had enough of the party. My feelings were hurt because Shanice stood me up for some gangsta brotha and all my boys had a girl to kick it with but me.

"Aw, look at the crybaby," I looked up and I saw Garfield, Cedric and Tony standing against the wall with some fly honeys.

"Ain't nobody crying," I tried to sound hard. Lord knows I wanted to punch him in the face but I wouldn't dare take that chance.

"Come on baby, don't act like that," Garfield put his hand up to my face like he was going to wipe a tear away. I quickly smacked it away which led to Tony and Cedric trying to run up on me.

This is what I was trying to avoid—getting jumped.

"Yo, what's up?" Allen came out from nowhere and approached Garfield. Garfield and Allen started walking around, shoulder to shoulder, daring each other to swing. Second and Brenda pulled Allen away from Garfield.

First, ol' boy steals my girl, now he's got my back with these Crips. I don't know whether I should steal off on him or thank you.

"He ain't worth it," Second kept pulling Allen away. His older brother, Love, came by too to help because Allen was about to fight Second to get at Garfield.

"I'll smoke all of you," Allen yelled.

I thought I was gonna crap in my pants. I could see the gun print in Garfield's pants. I don't know how he got past security, but I was scared of where the bullets were going to end up. Garfield, Cedric and Tony walked in the opposite direction. I later wondered if they were going to take it outside.

"What's good?" Carlton walked up to me.

"I'm alright…" I saw Carlton and the girl he was talking to walking toward me, "actually, I'm ready to go. I don't even want to be here anymore."

We looked at some of the other students that were getting their belongings and heading toward the door. I guess I wasn't the only one that wanted to go home.

"Aight man," Carlton said, "let m-e get this girl's number and then we can leave."

Calvin walked with his friend to get her belongings so that she could leave. To make matters worse, they put on some Mexican music and some of the kids started booing.

"That's messed up. We listened and danced to the black music…" I could hear Cisco complain.

"Yeah, how y'all gonna diss us like that?" another complained.

Nobody was trying to hear that music. For one, majority of us couldn't understand what they were saying. Two, nobody knew the dances that they were starting to take over the floor with. We weren't trying to diss their vibe, we just didn't understand it. Plus, the music we were playing before everyone was enjoying. I was watching Juan trying to keep up with his dance partner. I was reminded of how short he really was. I tried not to laugh, but I couldn't resist. Even Cisco, Texas, Arnez and the rest of their boys were laughing. I saw my father walking through the crowd trying to dance with the music. That made me laugh even more because my dad don't have no rhythm. I walked over to where he was at and tried to pull him off the floor. I had to stop him from embarrassing himself. My dad looked down at me pulling him away and was laughing, "you boys ready to go?"

"Yeah, we're ready," I heard Carlton reply. I could tell he was laughing.

We went and got our stuff so we could go. I was watching my dad watch the other students dance on the floor. "This music is the bomb!" he yelled, further showing his un-coolness.

"Let's go dad!" I yelled as I shook my head.

Carlton, Calvin and I followed my father to his car and we left the school. As we pulled off, we could hear that they were playing "Another Sad Love Song" by Toni Braxton. But it wasn't a sad love song; it was just depressing how the threat of violence always spoiled the mood.

And no time to play...

The boys and I finished up our sales for the day. We counted the money and did our split. I took the portion of the money that I was using to reinvest in the business and put it in a manila envelope. I hated walking home by myself with all the money. Normally, Calvin would be walking home with me, but he got sick and hadn't been to school the past week. That was the only thing I hated about everyone else living so close to the school. They didn't have to walk across 6th Avenue in that dangerous traffic. In the past month we've had three students get hit by cars either crossing 6th Avenue or Chambers Road.

The other reason I hated walking home by myself was because I never knew when Garfield or Freddie was going to pop up. Ever since Allen and Garfield almost got into a fight at the dance, I've been trying to avoid all the Crips. First of all, I didn't know Allen was a Blood until I met him. Secondly, I wasn't trying to get caught up in all that mess. Most of the people who are my age that claim Blood or Crip do so for the family ties. In many ways, it was the gift and the curse. It can be a gift when everyone in the set knows your family. The members look out for you; make sure you don't get in trouble. The curse was when the rival gang knows you are a relative, then you become fair game if anything goes down.

I crossed 6th Avenue with relative ease and when I get to the Albertson's Shopping Center, I saw Allen and Shanice coming out of the store. Shanice was all hugged up on Allen and trying to play with him. Allen sees me and acknowledges me. Shanice gives him a hug and a kiss and she walked to the car in the parking lot.

"Sup, l'il man?" Allen asked as he walked toward me. I looked around to make sure no one I know saw me talking to Allen.

"I'm good," I answered cautiously as I shook his hand.

"So you have been staying out of trouble lately?"

This little joker was nosy. Asking me all these questions liked he cared about me when he didn't. Nevertheless for my safety, I played along.

"Yeah man, what about you?"

Man, I don't know why I asked him that. I knew that Allen was into some type of trouble. Probably stole something from Albertson's.

"You know I stay out of trouble. What you getting ready to get into?"

"Bout to go home and do some work with my father."

Allen had a smile on his face as wide as a clown, and then just as if he was a shape-shifter, his face made a frown like a bulldog. I hope that I didn't say anything to make him mad.

"Shoot, I wish I had one of those," he rolled his eyes at me. I noticed him ball his fist and I kept my eyes on them because I wanted it to stay in his space and not in mine. I was trying to debate whether or not I could take Allen or not. I didn't want to have to fight him but I would at least try if I had to. Naw, let me quit playing, if Allen wanted to, he would beat me up.

"What's wrong kid? You look like you've seen a ghost."

"Nothing," was what I said. What I saw was Allen pulling out a gun and pistol whipping me.

"You know what? I've been watching you for a while. You run a tight operation with that candy shop you got at East."

"Thanks."

"You're one of those people who like money and I like that. We need more people like you. Shanice has been telling me about your operation."

I didn't think Shanice knew anything about what I do...let alone anything to tell him about it. I knew she probably told him I wanted to get with her, but that's all.

"But your operation lacks one thing I can offer."

I looked him in his eye, "what would that be?"

"Security." Allen spoke with confidence as if he had the answer for the solution I wasn't looking for.

"I got people for that."

He knew I was playing him. All I had was Second and Brenda. Darren was part of security too, he just didn't know it. Not to mention if my boys and I had to jump on somebody we would. But it never had to come to that and it was part of my job to see that it never would.

"You mean Second and Brenda?" he laughed at me. Who was I to think that I could put them two out like that? "Truth is, the only reason why nobody messes with Second is because everyone knows that is *my* boy, my best friend for life. So you see, you are already indirectly benefiting from having a relationship with me. I'll give that dude my life if I had to, but not everyone in my set will do the same. But if you side with me, I'll make sure you and your crew will receive full benefits."

"Side wit' you?"

"Damn boy, I know you not dumb. Become a Blood, that's what I'm talking about. You got the brains for it. You can keep doing you're little hustle and make money on a larger scale."

"Naw man, I can't do it," I said that too quick. I definitely didn't mean to let all my dominoes fall like that.

"Man, come on! Don't be no punk!"

"It's not about being a punk man. I just can't do it." It was too late for me to say anything different. I had already messed up so I might as well roll with it.

"Look dawg...I don't know what you got going on in that head of yours but what I'm bringing is real opportunity! First of all, I'm offering protection for life...you don't have to worry about Tony, Freddie, Cedric or Garfield trying to run up on you. Second, it's mad money to be made in our various business opportunities, all you gotta do is just choose one. And one of the best benefits is that you can get some mad trim."

"Trim? What's that?"

"The girl's yum-yum, man, pay attention! I see the way you be looking at Shanice and stuff. I know you want to hit it."

I just looked at him. He was bugging. I wasn't going to admit that I wanted to bone his chick. Not to his face anyway.

"Aight man, look at it like this...you join, I'll throw you some chicks that you can get your practice on. Then I'll let you break Shanice off a few times."

Oh my gosh, what did I get myself into? *Practice chicks*, who does that? "I don't want her if she's your girl."

"It's not like I'm a let you keep her. I'm just going to let you hit it once or twice."

He didn't even like Shanice the way I *liked* her. But she chose him so I had to respect that and let her figure out what she got herself into. I wouldn't share no chick with Allen anyway. With all them *practice chicks*, ain't no telling what he got and which *practice chick* he got it from. "I'm good man, I can't do it."

"What? You think we soft?" Allen got offended.

"Naw, it just don't fit with my plans."

Allen rolled his eyes at me and then balled his fist. My first instinct was to block it, but then I just stared him in the face, waiting to see what was gonna happen.

"Go on man. I ain't gonna mess with you. You got heart, but your heart needs to be guided in the right direction."

I just looked at him. I didn't realize my fist was balled and ready to be drawn until I looked down. Big mistake. I felt the wind come up as Allen brought his fist right to my face. At the last minute, I blocked it.

"Don't push your luck kid, go on!"

I backed away from Allen at first. I almost tripped on the sidewalk. I turned around and walked to my apartment. Truthfully, I could have taken him on his offer, but I wasn't trying to get caught up in no gang mess. Allen painted a really nice picture of what I wanted and what I could have. Lord knows I've been dreaming of banging Shanice since the moment I first met her. I could feel myself stirring and the blood leaving my brain just thinking about her. And what I would give for the opportunity to walk around in my Michael Jordan jersey. I got it two years ago and haven't worn it outside of the house yet. Everyone knows the Chicago Bulls are the best basketball team, but you won't catch anyone except those who are from Chicago wearing their uniforms. Just to have the right to wear red when I want to wear red, how I want to wear red…that was what I really want. But I don't want to join a gang to get that. My parents still pay all my bills and provide me a place to stay and some food to eat.

I'm saving my money so I can go to Morehouse or Howard. If I joined a gang, I would give all that up and I would constantly have to watch my back. I'm barely over five feet and I know that I would be too short for that. But most importantly, I would rather be free and alive than to be someone's prey and wonder when I'm gonna get gunned down.

But in the end it was all good...

"Martin!" my dad yelled as I was trying to wake up. Like the boy in the "Curtis" comics, I really wanted to sleep in, but my dad could be like his mama and whoop my tail if I didn't get up. "Martin!"

I sat up and forced my eyes to open. Dad was standing right over me. He looked like he was reaching for his belt. I wanted to back into the wall, but I got up instead. I rubbed my eyes so they could open wider.

"What is this?" I saw the paper that had flags around the edges. I was getting mad because my father knows I hate it when he snoops through my stuff. He read the letter out loud to reveal that we were having a race relations panel at our school. It's no secret that race issues were starting to become a problem at East. It seems like every other day we were trying to keep Arnez and Calvin from fighting. Both of them were hot heads, always trying to go at each other's throats. It seemed to be more of a problem with the sixth graders than it was any of the other students. This was one of the papers I should have thrown in the trash before I left the school. It was a community forum for both the students and parents and it was being sponsored by local leaders in the community.

"I don't want to go," I told him.

"I didn't ask you if you wanted to go. I asked you what it was?"

I wanted to exhale so bad, but I knew that would have ended with a smack across the face. "It's some information on a race relations forum at school."

"What makes you think *I* wouldn't want to go?" he questioned as he held the paper in my face.

"'Cause I don't want you to..." well, I didn't say that but I was thinking it. I looked at my father as he exhaled in disappointment. I got my clothes out and went to iron them in the living room. My father read the information on the flier and he placed it on the bed. He went to make a phone call and I was hoping that he wasn't calling Mom. The last I wanted was for her to show up too. I got dressed and walked to the kitchen so I could get something to eat, "you know to stay after school so we can be on time for this forum?"

I shook my head to let him know I understood. I was not happy about attending this forum. I didn't need to go listen to some speakers get on this Martin Luther King "We Shall Overcome" jive.

"Look little boy, you don't decide what I can and can't attend. Besides, your grandmother was Columbian."

"You mean I'm a Mexican, too?"

"No, get some ear swab and clean your ears. I said my mother was Columbian. I don't talk about my Hispanic heritage much because I don't know about it. I don't even speak Spanish. I was raised by my father's people. I wouldn't know my Mom's people if I seen them because I never met them."

Wow! All this time I had been dogging them Hispanic boys and come to find out that I am part Hispanic myself. I thought about all the mean and evil things I said and may have wanted to say and that my boys said. The racist's thoughts I felt about others who weren't black when I wasn't completely black. I wanted to know if my mother was part Hispanic as well.

"Is Mom Hispanic, too?"

"No. I'm sure she's not. Why, does it bother you to be part Hispanic?"

"No."

My father left the room and I walked over to where my encyclopedias were sitting on the bookcase. I researched Columbia to learn all I could.

***

I stayed after school so I could help set up the forum. I hadn't told any of my boys about my newfound heritage. Instead of hanging with my boys, I went to the library. I wanted to find out why I hated me so much. Normally, when people find out information about their family, they're happy about it. I wanted to understand why I wasn't. Moesha dropped her books next to mine and sat down. She picked up *Seize the Time* by Bobby Seale. I smiled because I read that book last year.

When I saw her this evening I noticed she was still reading the book.

"Sup Moesha?"

"Sup Martin. I didn't expect to see you here."

"I didn't expect to be here."

"So why did you come?"

"My dad wants to be here. He found the flier in my room and drew himself into it. Are you part Hispanic?"

"No, silly. I'm *all* black. Why'd you ask me that?"

I felt like I was the only person in the world other than my father and my brother that was going through this, "no reason."

"How come you didn't ask me to go to the Fall Dance?"

"I don't know. I didn't know you wanted to go."

"You were so caught up on trying to get that stuck up Shanice to go with you, you didn't even see if I had an interest in you."

"Well, how come you didn't ask me to go?"

"Because you're supposed to ask me, silly," my smile kind of fell, even though I wanted it to glide. Moesha's not that ugly but she ain't cute either. I'd give her a chance. Moesha moved to whisper in my ear, "you can get me something for Valentine's Day. It's only three months away."

Moesha skipped away and I heard her laughing. I turned around and saw Juan laughing and grinning at me.

"What's so funny?"

"You let that ugly girl kiss you, that's what's funny. Man, you can do better than that."

"Well, she's my girl."

"So I guess the sex is good?"

"What are you talking about?"

"You mean you don't know? Moesha is a l'il fast bro. She let that pretty boy on the track team hit it last year. Him and his boy."

"You mean Eric and DeVante."

"Yeah, them fake Jodeci cats."

I shook my head and started laughing, especially since I saw Eric and this fly looking honey come around the corner. Some of our parents started coming in and pretty soon, the cafe was full before you knew it. I wasn't surprised to see my dad showing off the new M.Walker products to the women in the audience. I swear that man don't ever miss a sale. I kind of wished I had brought my bag of goodies with me. When I looked at the rest of the crowd, I could see Texas and Cisco and some of their parents, too.

I listened to the man talk about "unity and the community" and all this other jive. I wished now more than ever that had lost that paper about today's meeting or at the very least thrown it in the trash. Then my dad got up to speak.

"When I was born out of wedlock, my mother was a fair skinned Columbian who came from a family who took after their Spanish and European ancestors. My father was a fair skinned black man. It's been said that because I came out with a little color, my mother didn't want me. So my father and his family raised me. Very little was said about my mother until I was seventeen and old enough to understand what was going on. So I researched my Columbian heritage; which served as a nice back drop to the Black Panther activist I had in my family. I even tried to track my mother down. But when I learned about the race issues and about how there are problems between the families with the darker skinned and lighter skinned members, I stopped.

"But we even have these problems within our own African American community. Lighter skinned brothers and sisters looked down upon their darker skinned relatives as inferior. Being lighter skinned got you into the right social organizations; a better job and even all, being lighter skinned brought along the perception that they were less of a threat.

"Not to be outdone, our darker skinned brothers and sisters took pride in being 'real' black folks. What is it they say, 'the blacker the berry the sweeter the juice,' or 'once you go black you can never go back.' All of these things can be derogatory and detrimental to our race.

"We enjoy being called French vanilla, butter pecan, chocolate deluxe; but we are quick to bring each other down instead of lifting each other up. Both black people and Hispanics suffer from complexion issues, and we take those attitudes and prejudices out on others. How we treat one another is a reflection of how we treat ourselves."

My father got applause all over the room. I saw Juan's father step up and approach the microphone.

"You've said the problem, but where is the solution?" he asked.

"The solution," my father answered, "is in acknowledging that we do this to ourselves. Acknowledging the power that is still behind the paper bag test and passing for white; all the while denying and being ashamed of *our* heritage. One of the advantages of being Hispanic is that we know where our people come from. Most if not all of our ancestors *chose* to come to America because we thought there was a better life and greater opportunities here. But for my black brothers and sisters...a good number of us still think Africa is a country and not a continent with over fifty countries. *We* don't even know if our people were Muslim, Catholic, or had their own religions.

"Another advantage is that Hispanics have built their own economy within America. They work the minimum wage jobs that black people can't or won't work and then they send the money back to their country to their families. The Hispanics shop at stores owned and operated by Hispanics; they buy their own newspapers; they demand that corporate America speak *their* language because they feel that their dollar is just as if not more than important than our own. Black people on the other hand still suffer from the crabs in the barrel effect. Minimum wage isn't good enough anymore. We still blame "the white man" for all of our ills and social problems. Since integration, we have forgotten about the black owned bookstores that *used* to give us knowledge. We bypass our stores because the prices are 'too high.' We buy our weave from Koreans; our jewelry from Iranians or Indians; we buy Japanese, Chinese, Italian and Mexican food. And the worst part is that we created all the fashion trends and the best music and we don't own the textiles or the record companies or the movie studios that profit from our image, our culture or our heritage."

"But that is not a Hispanic problem, that is the Negro problem," Cisco's father interrupted.

"It is everyone's problem because the dollars leave our community before they can come in. Hispanics have tasted racism in this country but black people have lived it. And we are still living it, in our minds. And until we can come out of it, it will be on everyone's mind. Look at all these Afro-Hispanics in Denver. Most Hispanics don't acknowledge them because they don't look white; they don't fit the stereotype of what a Hispanic or Latino is *supposed* to look like. Black people don't claim them because they call them 'Black Mexicans.' A lot of Hispanics have African heritage and ancestry, but they deny it in favor of the Spanish or Indigenous heritage because that is as close to being white as they are going to be."

"And that is the problem," Cisco's father yelled as he jumped from his seat, "everyone thinks we want to be white! We do not want to be white, we are Hispanic! We want to be respected just like everyone else in the country is respected. We are tired of being the butt of everyone's jokes!"

"I have to agree Mr. Little," Juan's father spoke up, "you are right about the black and Hispanic relationship and the need to improve that relationship so that both of us can benefit and survive in this country. But your assessment of us wanting to be white is offensive."

"That is true, but when was the last time an Afro-Hispanic was portrayed in the media as such. We are both to blame for that. Look at Mariah Carey, her father is both African & Venezuelan, but the white people think she is white. Just wait until she starts hanging out with rappers, and then she'll either be black or Hispanic, depending on who she hangs out with."

"But that is our problem, we see everything in black and white or with color," Juan's father said, "my wife is black and I am Mexican, but we try to avoid having our children choose one over the other. Yes, I speak Spanish in my house as does my wife, be we also support the African American community and the bookstore downtown and the other businesses you speak of."

The panelist took over the conversation and after giving out information on local agencies that work to the benefit of helping bridge the racial gap, the meeting was over. Juan's father came over to my father and shook his hand and they talked some more about their ideology and beliefs. I realized then that if older people could speak their peace and at the end of the day, put aside their differences, we should be able to do it too. My father continued to talk to the other adults and he collected some pamphlets and other information and then we left. In another week, Christmas Break would be upon us and I wonder how many people will have forgotten the conversation that took place today; or what would become of it.

For he sought a better way

I hated going to malls. I hate them because most people did nothing but stare at me all the time. I was always getting asked about the birthmark that encircled my eye. To some it looked like a crescent, but I was always asked if I had been beat up or abused. My mom said that she cried a lot when she had me and that is how my ugly mark came to be. All of the children in the mall point to it and ask what it is. My mom says that I should not let that bother me, but I can't help it. I get sick of the unwanted attention it draws every time I'm at the mall or in another public place.

"Sup Martin!" I turned around and saw Second and Brenda hanging out with Allen and some of the Bloods. My mom had this look on her face that said "make them go away."

"Sup Second, Brenda," I nodded my head to Allen and gave Second a pound and Brenda a hug. Allen threw up the peace sign and I smiled. He was trying to or was already kicking game to this girl he had hanging on his arm.

"That's your Mom?" Brenda asked as she waived at my mom and my brother.

"Yeah, I'm supposed to be Christmas shopping."

"Oh," Second responded. He grabbed Brenda by her waist and pulled her closer to him, "we're not gonna keep you. I just want to say what's up and to make sure that we're cool."

"I'm good…thanks for looking out."

"Anytime man," I gave Second pound again and I walked to catch up to my mother. Marcus had his hands out asking for some candy as we walked past the candy stand. The mall was packed for the Winter Break and there were a lot of children in the mall period. The line was long to see Santa Claus, but I was too old for that. Marcus wanted Mom to wait in the line but she gave him one of those looks that let him know that he was pushing her patience with him.

"You hanging out with gangs now?" Mom asked me.

"No…that is Second and Brenda from school. They do security for me from time to time. They're not gang members. Brenda's an honor student like me."

"Is that right?" My mom looked like she didn't believe me.

"Yes Mom."

"We'll talk about that when we get home."

I was not looking forward to Mom trying to talk to me when we got home. I knew that if there was going to be any kind of talking, it was going to be with her belt. Great, now that she though Second and Brenda are Bloods, she's probably going to assume that I want to be one. I could see it now, her using the fact that red is my favorite color after black. The fact that Second and I pounded. The fact that Allen was still smiling at me even as we walked away. On one hand, I didn't understand why Mom was tripping. Second wasn't a Blood and neither was Brenda. But the look on her face was more of one of disappointment rather than being upset. I was glad that Marcus had finally quit asking Mom for everything in the mall. Personally, I didn't care for Christmas all that much. I already knew about Mom and Dad playing all the usual holiday roles. I think the real reason why I hated Christmas was that it was starting to get too commercialized. It was supposed to be the season of giving, but it seemed like the season of getting. No one seemed to care about the fact that it was Jesus' birthday. If anything, we should have been buying Him presents. Instead, the grown folks have gone wild buying presents for their children. My friends would brag about the gifts they were getting from their parents. No one bragged about the church services or the plays they were going to see. Just last year, Dad and I saw two grown men fighting in the Wal-Mart over the last Barney doll. A *Barney doll!* I love you, you love me, but this whole mess is Cree-A-Z. You would think that Christmas time would bring more hugs and goodwill, but everyone wanted everything from everywhere except Goodwill.

"Mrs. Little!" I heard the most hateful voice in the world yell. I looked over to my left and I could see Garfield, Freddie and Cedric walking this way.

"Garfield," Mom was shocked. I don't know if Mom had spoke to Garfield's mom since she and my father had the talk about Garfield trying to get at me, "where is your mother at?"

Dumb question.

"She's a sleep. I'm just hanging out with my boys."

"At the mall?"

Garfield smiled and looked at me, "how's little man doing?" He put his hand on Marcus' head and patted it like he was a dog. I pushed his hand away and brought Marcus closer to me. Freddie looked like he wanted to say something but he kept his mouth shut.

"He's fine. I don't want you getting into trouble with your friends. You know as a young black man, the police have their eyes on you."

"I know," Cedric smarted off, "but when I show this," Cedric pulled out a huge roll of dollar bills, "they turn away."

"Cedric put that away," Garfield scolded, "you have to excuse my friend Mrs. Little he doesn't have any home training. But I did want to ask you about those pictures we took a while back."

"They turned out nice Garfield, your mom has them."

"She didn't tell me she got them."

"Well, I don't have them on me right now. Maybe if you come to the shop with your mom, I will show them to you."

"I'll do that."

"Come on Martin, Marcus."

Just as quick Mom scooped Marcus up and carried him as we made our way to the exit. I had all the bags she was carrying so I walked quickly to keep up with her pace. I looked up and Mom has this mixture of sadness and fear on her face. The bump bump sound in quickened repetitive patterns on the floor reminded me of a heart beat. I wondered if hers sounded like that. I looked behind me and I could see Garfield, Freddie and Cedric following close behind us. Freddie lifted up his shirt to reveal the gun he had concealed in his waistband. I was scared because I thought they were going to kill us in the mall. We stepped outside of the mall and in my excitement. I tripped and fell in the street.

"Martin!" Marcus yelled and my mother turned around to help me up. Garfield and his crew came running out of the mall.

"Martin, you okay man?" Garfield asked, continuing his act for my mother.

"Yeah, I'm fine," I got up and brushed the dirt and snow off of my clothes. I picked up my bags and Garfield was passing me the rest of the bags.

"Thank you Garfield," my mom said as I was snatching the bags from Garfield.

"You're welcome."

We walked the rest of the way to our car without incident. When we got in, I made sure to lock all the doors. Mom sped off out of the mall. We had seen Garfield walking around the mall and talking to some other hoods in blue.

"I don't want you hanging around him."

"I can't stand him anyway."

Mom gave me that look that said I shouldn't have gone there. It wasn't the fact that I spoke back that had me concerned, it was the fact that I was worried about my mom and Garfield was going to go the shop that was my biggest concern.

***

Mom must have really been shook up over Garfield at the mall. She called every beauty shop in the city trying to find where my father was. When she did find him, it didn't take but a few minutes for him to come home. I knew that I was going to end up in trouble based on the way my father looked at me when he got in. I didn't understand it; she saw Second and Brenda hanging out with some friends in the mall. Yeah, some of those friends were Bloods, but they were just hanging out. *Garfield* was the one that followed us in the mall. *Garfield* was the one that confronted her about some pictures she took. *Garfield*, not Second. Yeah, Second's boy was a Blood, but that was his boy, not him.

I wonder if Mom has talked with Garfield's mother since she and my dad *supposedly* talked a few months ago. I don't see how Garfield's mother could not see her son for what he was. No I get it, Garfield's mother was in denial. She doesn't want to believe that her "baby" is out there doing all that mean and cruel stuff to people. I know she doesn't believe that she raised him to be that way, and deep down inside, I'm pretty sure that was the case, but Garfield was a monster. I know that was a mean thing to think of someone and a meaner thing to say it but it was the truth. I feel sorry for her. I hoped that she had some other children that she could be proud of. My dad walked into the room interrupting my train of thought.

"You hanging out with Bloods?" he asked me.

"No, my friend's friend is a Blood." I defended myself.

"Sound like he's your friend to me."

My dad was skeptical. I could tell that my mother amplified the situation to talk more about how close Second and Brenda were to me than the issue of what happened with Garfield.

"Dad it's not like that at all. Second is a really cool guy. Remember, he's the one that was in the fifth grade with us last year but got moved back into his right grade. The real short guy."

Dad laughed and shook his head. He must have remembered the time Second and Franklin got into it last because Franklin was talking about how short he was. If it weren't for my father scooping Second up like he was a toddler, Franklin would have caught a beat down.

"Does Second have any other friends?"

"His girlfriend is Brenda."

"I remember her. Her older brothers run track for Hinkley. Does she still dress like a little boy and stuff?"

"Yeah," I laughed because I couldn't remember the last time I seen Brenda in any girl's outfit. She always acted and looked like a little tomboy that was why I hired her just to deal with the girls. Don't let it fool you. She could hang with the fella.s too. "But Dad, if I thought Second was a gang member, I wouldn't be using him on my team."

"I know, but sometimes people don't see the person you are, they see the company you keep. Second is putting himself in a dangerous position hanging out with whoever it is he's hanging out with. I know his mama would be very upset if she knew that her son was hanging out with hoodlums and hoodrats."

"Yes sir."

"You just be careful of the company you keep. You know I love you, but you do anything that lands you in juvie, you'll be staying there with your bad friends."

"Yes sir."

My father left the room and Marcus came in. He wanted me to play toy soldiers with him and I did. I sat on the floor and let Marcus beat my soldiers to smithereens. But I wasn't thinking about playing with Marcus, I was evaluating my crew. Calvin was the only one who really could get me in some trouble. At the same time, Calvin was one of the funniest guys I knew. It's almost like there are two Calvins; the fun and almost selfish one will come out most of the time. But do something to make that boy mad and you'll see a whole new creature. And nobody brings out that other side of him better than Arnez. Personally, I think Arnez likes the fact that he can get under Calvin's skin. Juan and I have warned that boy several times about picking at Calvin like that, but Arnez is just as hotheaded and stubborn as Calvin was. And maybe that was why they don't get along...they are so much alike 'til it ain't even funny.

Some things are worth fighting for...

Christmas was nice. I got a new CD player for the room and a bunch of CD's to go with it. I was surprised to see Snoop Doggy Dogg's *Doggystyle* wrapped under the tree. I knew that my dad was behind that one. I also got some old Public Enemy, Will Smith and Doug E. Fresh CD's along with the latest music. My brother got a lot of the toys that he wanted and as usual, he had them all over the floor in the room. Sammie and Lester came over a few times over the holidays and Sammie, Casey and my brother started terrorizing the rest of us. Well, Sammie wasn't as bad but Casey and Marcus together would scare all the lions and tigers and bears out of the wild.

Moesha called me two times over the holidays. I guess her family went to Philadelphia. She was talking about the long drive and how she wished they could have flown instead. She also talked to me about celebrating Kwanza and what each day meant and lighting candles and stuff. My mother's people live in Tennessee and it has been a long time since we visited them for Christmas. I would have wanted to go see them, but I don't control any situations here.

Now that we are back from break, there were a lot of things I wish we could have left in 1993 as we moved into 1994. Number one, I don't want the Hispanic guys trying to sell candy *ever* again. It didn't take long for my crew to wrestle control away from them because they weren't serious about it but I was serious about mines. Number two; I wanted

Garfield to stay as far away from East Middle School as possible. I know that is reaching, but what could he possibly want with a bunch of twelve, thirteen and fourteen year olds? I mean, I know he is not that much older than us but he is too old to be hanging around us. And finally, it would be nice if Calvin could finish the school year without fighting anyone.

"Calvin!" Arnez yelled from the hallway in the cafeteria. "Calvin!"

There went my wish. I knew before I stepped foot on campus that Calvin was bound to fight a few people before the year was over with. We hadn't been back from Christmas break three days and already he's looking at possibly a one week suspension. Calvin turned around and looked at Arnez. Calvin's face was beet red...no, more like strawberry. I have never seen Calvin this mad or upset before. I wanted him to walk away and just let the whole situation go, but a small part of me wanted them to fight and get it over with. Arnez and Calvin had always had it in for each other. Truthfully, it may be better this way, for them to fight. Calvin started running down the hallway and I was going to stop him from getting in Arnez' face but Juan and Darren was holding me back.

"Let them fight..." Juan looked at me sadly. I don't think Juan meant that but something was using him to hold me back, "let them fight. Because we will never work together if they don't fight now."

By time we got there, I felt the force of Arnez' fist fly pass me as he landed a blow square on Calvin's jaw. Not to be outdone, Calvin through a series of blows that landed on Arnez' face and body. The girls in the hall were screaming and the Hispanic boys started forming a semi circle on one side and my friends started forming a semi circle on the other side. My stomach started flying up and down as Arnez and

Calvin fought like lions trying to protect their territory. The circle seemed to be growing wider as Arnez and Calvin needed more room to work out their aggression. I looked each of the Hispanic boys in their eyes and each of them had hate in their eyes, and I felt them glaring at me. As the circle started to close, everyone started pushing and shoving. I was a little scared because I didn't want to be involved in no war. Juan and Trey looked like they were ready to throw some blows. Darren reached in and grabbed Calvin and Cisco pulled Arnez back. The teachers were coming, I knew that much...but we ran home as soon as we could so that neither boy would get caught.

Outside, the sun was crying very hard and as we ran, the leaves started attaching themselves to our clothing. We stopped at Lester's house and we were hoping that his mother wasn't home. Lester and Calvin went to the bathroom and the rest of us waited in the living room. We could hear Calvin cursing and yelling at Lester who was trying to help him clean his bruises. The doorbell rang and all of us looked at each other. Juan went and looked out the window and then he closed it back fast.

"Who is it?" Trey asked.

"Cisco and Texas. I can't tell if Arnez is with them or not," Juan responded.

The knocking on the door got louder and we thought we heard some kicking. There was some yelling outside and some tapping on the door.

"Man, we can't be fighting in Lester's house," Franklin balled his fist, "we are going to have to take this outside."

Juan opened the door and Franklin ran out from behind him. Everyone else ran out of the house and we looked at the boys.

"Look holmes, we come in peace," Cisco stared Franklin in his face, "I'm not trying to start no war, but we all knew that Arnez and Calvin were going to fight sooner or later. Now back up out of my face Frankie!"

If there was one thing in the world that Franklin hated, it was being called Frankie. Franklin felt that Frankie was the feminine version of his name and that anyone who used it was trying to imply that Franklin was gay. Franklin backed away, his fist were still tighten and ready to serve their duty if needed.

"Where is Arnez?" I tried to break the tension.

"Ra-Ra got him held up somewhere. But we can worry about that later. Look, we don't need to be fighting amongst ourselves because if you guys haven't noticed, more Crips started hanging out in the area. We barely got away from the fight circle because they kept pushing us in. Now, I don't know whether they were trying to get at Calvin, Arnez or both of them…"

"Arnez?" Ray asked, "what would the Crips want with Arnez?"

"Arnez' sister is sleeping with one of the Bloods from Park Hill. Just like Calvin is y'alls little hot head, Arnez is ours. Quiet as it is kept, Arnez been walking around claiming Blood and he starting to get us into some things. Look, I don't know how to say it, but we are going to need y'alls help."

"I've been noticing that, too. I mean, Garfield has been hanging around too much for my comfort," Juan complained.

Lester and Calvin came out of the house and we saw Arnez and Ra-Ra coming up the street. Before anyone could say anything, we started hearing "Murder Was the Case" being blasted from an old Cadillac that seemed to be flying down the street. Before anyone could think to do anything, we ran to the house and fell to the ground. In that moment, I knew that God existed because the bullets were flying over us. One hit the window and we could hear the car screeching. I was scared to look up, but I felt my body being dragged across the grass. At that moment, I had wondered if I had been hit, but I didn't feel any burning or tingling sensation. I turned around and a pair of hands grabbed my shirt and lifted me up. I felt a few inches taller as I looked Garfield in his dark chocolate eyes. If there ever was a moment that I wished I was a little bit taller, this would be it. I tried to feel for the ground with my feet, but I accidentally kicked him in the shin. Garfield threw me on the ground and I stayed there, look up at his blue jean uniform.

"Damn it," Garfield yelled as he kicked me in my ribs. I felt nachos and Twinkies making a U-Turn in my stomach and attempt to come up from my throat. "Where the hell is Calvin?!"

I looked around for a minute and I saw everyone in our crew but Calvin. I looked at the house for a minute and with the door being closed I assumed, no, I prayed he was inside in the basement. I looked up at Garfield and shook my head. I really didn't know where Calvin was. Garfield was not satisfied as he lifted me up from the ground again. At that moment, I developed a sudden hatred for merry-go-rounds and other amusement park rides.

"Let me tell you something. You tell that little punk bee-otch that he better have my money or else he won't live to see thirteen!"

Garfield punched me in the chest again and ran to the Cadillac. The Cadillac's wings spread again as it hopped on the street, about ready for take off. I didn't see any of that as

I was squirming on the floor, trying to decide if I was going to expel my lunch or not. My throat was burning as the sweet taste of NowAndLaters started to turn sour. I wished that my stomach would make up its mind if it was going to come up now or later so I could better be prepared.

"You okay man?" Darren asked as he and Texas were lifting me up.

"I think I'm going to be okay," I still tried to feel where the contents of my lunch were.

The door to Lester's house opened and Calvin yelled for everyone to come inside. I looked around the other neighborhood houses and I didn't see anyone at the windows, trying to see the aftermath of the neighborhood's drive by shooting. Then again, I hoped that no one was near the windows when everything went down.

"How did you get in the house?" Lester said.

"I heard them coming and I ran in. I was praying for y'all out there."

We all walked into the house and Lester led us down to his room in the basement. He had pictures of Jordan and Magic Johnson all over his room. I laid at the foot of the bed so I could help my stomach make up it's mind what it wanted to do. I could hear the boys' excitement about our first drive by and how they barely missed bullets. How they wished they had guns so they could blast back.

"Calvin, how much money did you steal from Garfield? No, tell me how you stole the money from Garfield to begin with? I need to pick that up," Arnez asked with excitement in his voice.

"I didn't steal nothing from that fool! Well, I got his girl for a few dollars while she was paying for her order at McDonalds. I just rolled up on her, snatched the money out of her hand and I was off. I didn't care about her being Garfield's girl or anything. I saw an opportunity to take a little bit from them."

"Damn Calvin, you are bold as hell," Ra-Ra yelled, laughing, "I don't think I'd ever have the balls to do that."

"But you know what? I don't even think all of this was worth it because even though I got like twenty dollars, it doesn't bring Carla back."

We sat around and thought about our situation at hand. The day had finally come when my friendship with Calvin would be put to the test. Of course, I was ready to take a bullet for him, or even die for him. I already got beat up for him so that was only a natural progression.

"I'm tired of the Crips telling me what I can wear, where I can sit and what I can and can't do with my time," Darren said, "but I ain't big enough to fight all of them."

"Who said you got to be big?" Texas asked as he started pacing the room, "look at us, sitting around here like some broke eses? We need to join forces and fight these mugs together. We could be like the resistance movement in *Number the Stars*. Standing up for what we believe in. Isn't that what Mr. Shakur was talking about in class today?"

"Yeah," I surprised myself. I had already read the book several times and even admired the girl's older sister for standing up against the German in World War II. But we were not defiant nineteen and twenty year olds who could get access to guns and talk back to Germans. We were eleven and twelve year old boys who were barely capable of pulling a trigger on a gun, more or less being able to defend ourselves against an army of Crips. There were thousands of them and maybe twenty of us. Majority of us were around my height, give or take an inch. How the hell did we expect to take on a powerful and large gang of Crips? We were one set of sixth graders at one school...what would make the other sixth graders at other schools join us if we did decide to do something as stupid as this? Wait a minute! We weren't deciding to do something as stupid as this...were we?

To get what you want out of life...

Calvin and I were walking to school and we made a pit stop to Albertson's. Calvin claimed he wanted to get some chips. I don't know why I agreed to this stop. I had money to make and the five to ten minutes we were late was going to be five to ten minutes we didn't have to sell candy. When Calvin and I got in the store, we saw this fly honey in this dark blue and white outfit. She looked like she could have been hanging out with Salt 'N' Pepa or in the latest Snoop Doggy Dogg video.

"That's Garfield's chick," Calvin's mischievous grin formed on his face.

"So, she don't got nothing we want. Besides man, you need to leave her alone man, you messing with her is what got us shot at in the first place. I don't know her and she don't know me and it needs to stay that way."

"Well, she knows me, and she knows my sister. They used to roll together before she met Garfield."

"And she's with Garfield now?" I almost blew my cover. I had kept the fact that Garfield confessed to killing Carla in the back of my mind and I was *this* close to blowing my cover.

"Yep. It's funny how she stopped coming by when Carla died. When Carla was alive, she used to come by all the time, even if Carla wasn't around. Sleepovers and stuff. Now she sees me or Carlton or Casey, she turn the other way. Watch this," Calvin walked up to the girl and tapped her on the shoulder. The lady at the register was giving her change. She drops the change, as she is shocked that Calvin is tapping her. She quickly turns around.

"Calvin," she yelled and smiled, "you always playing with me. When you gonna give me my money back? I know that was you that ran up on me and got me for my twenty dollars."

"Girl, you know I ain't do you like that. Besides, I haven't seen you in a minute Nicole."

"You know I hate it when folks call me Nicole, call me Cola."

"Well Cola, when are you going to come by the house again?"

Cola looks around. It was clear that she was annoyed by him as she starts to pick up her pace and walk out of the store.

"Why are you running?" Calvin called out as they walked out of the store.

"I'm not running. I am late. I was supposed to meet my man, we got things to do. I'll catch up with you later."

We watched as Cola ran across the street and waited on the bus. Calvin looked at me with that same mischievous grin that he had on his face earlier. I knew then that the boy was up to something.

"I know she was in on killing my sister," Calvin tossed his bag to me, "now she is going to pay."

I wanted to call out his name and run after him, but Calvin was a lot faster than I was. He was also stubborn and very set in his ways. I just knew that what was to come next was not going to be pretty. I hadn't been paying attention, but Calvin had pulled out some rocks that he must have picked up earlier from our walk. Calvin was always throwing rocks at something or someone. Now, he was standing in the middle of Chambers Road, throwing rocks at the girl.

"You trick! You killed my sister!" Calvin yelled as he flew to the bench and began pouncing on the girl. It was like watching the Incredible Hulk. He pulled her hair and was throwing her head into the bench. He then snatched her purse and kicked her before he ran across the street. He started throwing her personal items all over the street. He took her money and put it in his pocket. "I'll kill you later!" He barked as he caught up with me and ran toward the school. At that moment, I wanted to go home. I didn't feel safe going to school, but how was I going to explain to my father that I let Calvin beat up on some girl. But I was more scared of being at home by myself while dad was out working. Besides, someone needed to stay with Calvin because he has really lost his damn mind.

***

The rest of the school day, I was on alert. Calvin on the other hand was acting like nothing had happened and was doing his thing as usual. I didn't see how he could have done it. Juan and Darren noticed something different about Calvin, too. Calvin was thought he was O-Dog from *Menace II Society*. For better or for worse, we played along with him because we really didn't want Calvin to get into any more fights. One thing I did notice was that Freddie, Cedric or Tony were nowhere to be found. Normally, they had something smart to say to us and were trying to get at us for one thing or another.

When school got out, we walked with Lester to go get Sammie. Sammie had been begging Lester to let him hang out with us all day, and we promised Lester that Sammie could hang out with us today. We waited off of Elkhart's property for the elementary school students to get out of class. As usual, Carlton was macking to some chick. This one didn't look half bad at all. She was a nice caramel looking sista that could have passed for the older version of Rudy from *The Cosby Show*. We were listening and laughing at Carlton because as much as he thought he was cool, we knew he was corny. He was bragging about how big he was and what he was going to do to her when they had a few minutes alone. He grabbed her hand and invited her to feel it, but she slapped him and we started rolling. Didn't nobody wanted to touch his nasty thing. He needed to learn to control his hormones.

"Clarice! What are you doing?" Freddie yelled as he started approaching Carlton and the girl.

"We ain't doing nothing Freddie. Carlton and I are just hanging out."

I don't know why she was lying, she just smacked him a minute ago.

"Yeah man, we ain't doing nothing. Clarice and I are just having some conversation, that's all."

Freddie got in Carlton's face like he wanted to fight him. Freddie looked him up and down and he walked away. We were still laughing at Carlton when the school bell rang and the elementary kids were bursting out of school as if they were running to an amusement park. We spotted Sammie in no time as he started running toward us.

"Aww..." Juan said, "look at little Lester."

"Let's hope he doesn't get chubby like him," Darren teased.

"Both of y'all can shut up!" Lester scooped Sammie up carried him on his shoulder. Carlton walked over to where we were at and took Sammie down from Lester's shoulder.

"Are you Big Calvin?" Sammie asked.

"Nope, I'm his older brother."

"That's what I meant. I'm Little Lester because I'm his younger brother. You are Big Calvin because you are his older brother."

"Is that right? Well you need to call him Little Carlton, cause the little boy wants to be just like me."

"Whatever," Calvin said as we laughed again.

"Yeah, you're right," Carlton owned up, "you could *never* be me."

Calvin pushed him and Carlton pushed him back. Carlton put Calvin in a headlock and started rubbing his knuckles on his head.

"Yo, hold that boy right there!" Garfield yelled as we saw Freddie, Cedric and Tony following behind him. Carlton let Calvin go and stepped in front of him.

"What's up man? What do you want with my brother?"

"Look dog, you need to step out of this because Little Man and I got some business. Putting his hands on my girl, I'm show him some thangs…"

"Calvin didn't touch your girl! And you not gonna touch him!"

"Look you fake Fresh Prince looking punk," Garfield was getting in Carlton's face now. My boys and I started to rush on Garfield because we were going to have Carlton and Calvin's back. Tony stepped back and pulled out a gun on us and we stepped back.

"What y'all think y'all doing? You not going to roll up on us while we handling business," Tony yelled as we started to back up.

"This is the fool that tried to get at my girl!" Freddie yelled as he, too, got in Carlton's face.

"Oh word!" Garfield pushed Carlton and Calvin almost fell down. Carlton was trying to get up because he was about to trip and Freddie rushed him. Garfield and Cedric rush Carlton as they started jumping on Carlton and Calvin. Tony kept the gun leveled on us so that we would move.

"Move back some!" Tony instructed and as we moved back. One eye was on the gun and the other was Carlton and Calvin getting they butts beat. Carlton tried to fight all three of them but he could only do so much. Calvin was trying to push on Freddie but he wasn't a match for them either. Finally, Garfield came from behind Calvin and scooped him up and body slammed him in the grass. I felt the vibrations of his landing trickle down my spine cause for a moment there, I thought that was me. Tony dragged Calvin to where we standing and point the gun at him. Garfield went back and they started stomping on Carlton. The elementary children that had run up to watch the fight had begun to wish they hadn't. They were screaming as they saw Tony move the gun from right to left.

The Hispanic boys walked over to the school and they pushed themselves in front of the elementary school children. I looked back at the building to see if any teachers or even better if the police were coming. That would have been too good to be true and when I saw more children coming to watch the fight, I wasn't even disappointed.

"All of y'all sit down!" Garfield barked as he snatched the gun from Tony. We did as we were told and we spread out as Garfield started coming closer and closer to us. I thought that my life was going to end right there as Garfield started coming closer to me. I wanted to shake my head; a part of me wanted to run but I was still as a statue. I looked over to my left and I could see Calvin sitting up, a little conscious. I looked back at Garfield and the gun as he smacked me across the face with it.

"That's for snatching them bags out of my hand, you little punk," he said as I got up. He had the gun pointed at my face and I could feel my soul crawling away from my body. "Freddie, get they bags and their money. We're gonna do this just like they did my girl."

Freddie was snatching bags off of all of us and Cedric and Tony pulled out more guns to control all of us. Garfield started talking to himself, asking out loud who was it that robbed his girl and put a scar on her face. I knew the answer, but I wasn't going to give it to him. I knew he knew the answer, but I knew that he wanted to do something more drastic. As Garfield started getting crazier, we all started backing away from him...or at least we tried.

"Stand up fools!"

I saw little horns growing from the top of Garfield's head and if I cared to look a little closer, I might have saw a tail or two. Garfield looked like an animal; a being with no compassion or respect for life. I could tell that he was a killer and that he would kill again. I had begun to mourn the life of whoever it was he was going to take in the next few moments. As much as I wanted to believe this could end peacefully, I already knew that the end would be coming. Garfield was swinging the gun around the playground like a mad man. Carlton lay on the floor unconscious and Calvin looked a mess.

"Aw, what's up! You guys think you are so big and bad selling candy. Stealing from my girl, now see, I don't know which one of you smart fools thought that was a good idea but I'm going to show you," Garfield yelled as he kicked Carlton again. Cedric and Tony were pointing guns at all of us while Freddie was running through our bags and taking our candy and our money. Good thing today was a slow day and I made the decision to make my deposit yesterday. I was already trying to think of a good lie I could tell my mother to convince her that I would need for her to go to the store for us again. When Freddie started opening the candy and throwing it all over the playground, I knew this was going to go where it didn't need to go. Arnez and Ra-Ra looked like they were about to make a mistake in their pants. "So I am going to ask you guys one more time, where is my girl's money?"

"Look man," Lester stepped closer to Garfield. I was scared because Garfield continued to swing the gun around back and forth, pointing it at each of us. My worst fear was that it was going to go off and hit one of us, "we got more than enough money to replace whatever you feel Calvin stole from your girl. Just take all we have and I promise you that none of us will ever go near your girl again."

"You know what? I could do that. I could take all your money because this is at least triple what that little runt over there stole from my girl. But it is the principle of the issue. I don't come up on y'all trying to stop y'all from selling candy on my property, even though y'all are trespassing. And I don't expect you to steal from me, my girl or anyone else on my team...or break any of my rules!"

Garfield walked over to Lester and smacked him with the gun. Lester floated a few feet backward and tripped over his untied shoe laces. Garfield picked him up from the ground with one fist and raised him to the sky. I didn't think anyone would ever do that to Lester but the guy's arm looked like Mike Tyson's on steroids.

"Let go of my brother!" Sammie yelled as he ran toward Garfield trying to kick or hit on him. Lester tried to push Sammie out of the way before Garfield could kick him.

"Raise up you little…"

BOOM! The gun went off and we ducked to the ground for cover. I looked up and my eyes met with Juan's and we were watching Lester and Sammie tackle Garfield. Time slowed down like images from the film reel and I saw every millisecond flash before my eyes. Sammie had fallen down but ran back up to bite Garfield on his leg. Sammie threw three or four good punches to Garfield's crouch area, probably meaning to hit him in the leg. Garfield had dropped Lester and in the process, Lester got a good lick in his jaw. Calvin ran up and kicked Garfield in the back. Cedric raised his gun in the air and pulled the trigger, making everyone fall down again. Sammie ran up to Garfield, looking like a miniature David against a super-sized Goliath and he started throwing punches again. With the gun in his hand, Garfield pushed Sammie backward again. Sammie landed on his butt and he got up again. Lester pulled on Garfield's other arm and Garfield smacked him with the gun and Lester fell off like a fly. Sammie also received a hit in the face when Garfield's arm came around. Garfield's finger pulled the trigger. The bullet tip-toed to Sammie's head, entered it's skull after one knock and came out the back of Sammie's head. Sammie's eyes rolled to the back of his head and at that moment he fell down for the very last time. I knew he was dead.

"Damn!" Garfield got up and slowly walking away from us.

"You shot the kid?" Tony questioned as he ran up to Sammie's body and turn him over, face down.

"The gun went off," Garfield said, "he shouldn't have run up on me. None of these kids should have run up on me!"

"Oh man!" Freddie said putting the last little bit of money that he had taken from some little girls in his pocket.

Another shot rang out as Garfield, Freddie, Tony and Cedric started to run off the campus, "y'all didn't see nothing! You hear me! Y'all didn't see nothing!"

I thought I saw a tear roll down Garfield's eye, but gangstas don't cry. I looked at Sammie's body and the puddle of blood that was coming out of his head. Lester had picked him up and started cradling him as if he were a baby. He started singing the song that was at the end of the *Sister Act 2* movie. Joyful, joyful Lord? That was a joke. What kind of God would allow such a vicious act of violence to happen to a five year old? I looked at Sammie's body again and I was jealous of him. I wished at that very moment that I could touch him and the bullet wound would move from his head to mine. God had no right allowing Garfield to kill a child much younger than me. All those middle schoolers on the playground and He takes a kindergartner. Joyful Lord? I was not adoring watching Lester and the rest of us cry over Sammie's body, our hearts broken right before our eyes. Joyful Lord? The police arrived and the emergency team arrived a few minutes too late to save us. At that moment, I hated the police because they were supposed to be here to protect us, instead they were late. Probably too scared to come on the playground…they probably didn't believe that the Crip would really kill a five year old, but Sammie would make the sixth four or five year old that the Crips had killed in four months. Joyful Lord? I hated Him for allowing this to happen and I hated Him even more because He didn't allow any of the bullets to hit me. Three shots were fired and not one of them could hit me. One could come and go through Sammie's head but He couldn't find a way to make one pierce me in my head. Fill us with the light of day. Yeah, the light of day was shining bright as ambulances and police cars speed off with Sammie's body and Lester somewhere in tow. To show you how great the Aurora Police Department was, they left all of us children still stunned on the parking lot, after asking us all these questions about what happened and they didn't offer one of us a ride home. The school buses were gone and all of us now had to run across Sixth and Chambers in real rush hour traffic. Joyful Lord? You know what, after all of this I don't believe in Him any more. Now where was the joy in that?

Some hits a man has to take...

I woke up the morning of Sammie's funeral. Marcus was crying because he couldn't understand why the boy he was playing with just a week ago was not coming back. I sat up in the bed and I didn't feel like leaving. Marcus gave me a hug and I held him tight for dear life. I wished that I had held Sammie as tight as I was holding Marcus because maybe he would still be with us.

We had grief counselors calling us and trying to get us to "deal" with Sammie's death. I didn't want to "deal" with anything. I wanted the little boy back! I wanted the fun boy with big, bouncy curls with freckles begging Lester to play with us back. I wanted to play with him. Instead, I had been crying off and on for the past week, remembering Sammie. Remember how he dressed up at our soccer game and sold candy for us. Remembering how Lester and I would pick him up from school almost every day and him telling us how the other children at Elkhart were. I wanted to watch the little boy that was full of life become alive again.

My father came in the room and he sat down on my bed and he hugged me. He rocked me like I was a little baby and he hugged me. He was telling me how everything was going to be okay. I knew that it would be a long time before things ever got to be okay. I had dreams of Marcus, Casey and Sammie going to middle school and not having to worry about getting shot at or what color they could wear or any of the things my friends and I had to worry about. I had dreams about Sammie and Lester having fun and doing the normal things brothers do.

I finally got up and took a shower and put on the outfit that my mother had laid out for me. Sammie's parents had requested that no one wear all black to the funeral. I personally wanted to wear red but I knew not to even ask. Dad was wearing a silver and blue sweater and Mom had on a green and gold turtle neck with some slacks. Marcus looked like a miniature version of my father with the silver and blue sweater and black pants. As for me, I had pulled out this grey, blue and black sweater with diamond patterns all over it. After I finished putting on my clothes, my mother had to force me to eat something. I ended up eating a bagel and an apple. I really wasn't hungry.

When we stepped out of the house Calvin, Casey and his mother were waiting on us in their car. We were going to meet some of the other parents at Elkhart and then drive in procession to the church where Sammie's service was being held. Carlton was in the hospital for three days after Sammie's murder and he wasn't well enough to go to Sammie's funeral. His father stayed at home with him so that he could make sure Carlton was being taken care of.

We got to the school and we could see the black limousine carrying Lester and his parents in front of the school. It was hard walking on Elkhart grounds after all that had happened. I started having flashbacks of the bullet entering Sammie's head.

Patti LaBelle's "I Don't Like Goodbye's/Somewhere Over the Rainbow" from one of her concerts was blasting in the car. I could see an older man with curly red hair shaking other grown folks' hands. I knew he was Sammie's father. I looked for Lester and his mother but I think they stayed in the limousine. I recognized some of the other kid's parents and cars. When it was time to go, we followed a long line of cars to the church.

There were so many people who had come to pay their respects to Sammie. Many of the teachers I remembered teaching me in elementary school were crying many tears. Even the ones whom I had thought were mean and heartless showed the expression of hurt and sorrow on their faces. A lot of children from Sammie's class and in the neighborhood were in attendance as well. Everyone had on something colorful and many came with Bibles in their hands. I had felt like I had walked into the middle of a church service.

The funeral was long…real long. My back was sore from sitting in the wooden benches for the long period of time. I looked around to see Calvin with this menacing look on his face. The tears were rolling down his cheek so fast that one could hear them land on his jacket. Maybe that was because the room was so still and quiet. We were all upset and angry that Sammie was dead. This was another senseless murder where a kindergartener or a first-grader was getting killed. The Crips had reached a new low murdering all of these little children for no reason at all. And at the moment I hated God because I could not understand why He didn't take me. Maybe saying that I hated God was a little strong. I was just disappointed in Him. I mean, didn't I have a right to be upset that all these children were dying and it seemed to me that He wasn't doing anything about it? They say He has His reasons and I want to know why? What do you need a five year old for? Why did he have to take the bullet? Couldn't You have taken him in his sleep or something? He did not have to go out like that. I hope I or my brother or no one else had to go out like that ever again. But God is God and one day I would learn to understand Him.

My mom was passing me a tissue. I hadn't realized that I had been crying, too. I needed a bucket so I could barf in, that was what I was feeling. I wish that God would just kill me slowly and let my soul pour out into the trash can. I mean…that was what He was letting happen to all those little children. As the children's choir sang my soul stirred. My heart tuned into the beat of the drum and became one with it. My muscles seemed to be dancing to the rhythm of the piano and my eyes fluttered with every vibration from the guitar. Everyone else's eyes were on the sparrow but mine were on that doll faced boy who lied in the coffin. Their parents looked like ghosts and his mom passed out when they closed the coffin. She almost dropped the baby she was carrying in her arm. I felt the most sorry for Lester…losing his brother like that. And yet I felt sorry for myself because there was nothing I could do to bring him back.

***

Surprisingly, Lester's mother let him leave their house and hang out with us at Chuck E. Cheese. That was the only thing all of our parents could think of to try to keep our spirits up. There were others who came and apologized to Lester for the loss of his little brother. Some cried while others were speechless…and still are speechless.

"I want to get those punks back, but I don't know how," Lester broke our silence. We were trying to enjoy our cheese pizzas but most of the pizza slices were still on the wheel.

"Are you sure you are up for it? Say the word and I'll be ready to bust a c…" Calvin got riled up but stopped. I think he caught on to what he was saying and chose to be cautious over his words.

"I want to bust a cap in their asses. Garfield, Cedric, Tony, Freddie…all of them Crips man, I want to get them! But where am I going to get a gun?" Lester responded.

"Who said we needed a gun?" Arnez slid into our booth and reached for a slice of pizza, "I can get a knife or scissors and stab him."

"Man we can't use no knife…remember Lisa got a year suspension for accidentally bringing her dad's pocket knife to school last year. That is still ridiculous and so unfair," I suggested, also attempting to eat the slice of pizza I had on my plate, "Lisa almost got expulsion for an accident. But Garfield, Freddie and the rest of the Crips come to school freely and wreck havoc on all of us and the principals and stuff turn the other way. It's almost as if they don't want to see it."

"Yo man," Calvin interrupted. "Remember that book we were reading in class…*Numbers* something."

"*Number the Stars.*" Darren corrected.

"Yeah, *Number the Stars*…and now with that *Soul on Ice* book that Mr. Shakur got us reading. I'm thinking we could put together a movement just like they did," Calvin went on.

"A movement?" Ra-Ra questioned, he was straightening up in his seat. "We are not old enough to be starting a movement."

"And fourteen year olds are not old enough to be Crips but they got them. Why not start a movement and take over the whole school? Why we got to wait to be eighth graders before we can do something? We can start right now."

"Hold up holmes," Texas stated. "Those people in *Number the Stars* and the Black Panther Party had guns and stuff to fight back with. We don't have that. Yeah, plus they were older."

"And I keep telling you, we don't need that," Calvin argued as he was finishing his pizza. "We are not just going to run up on some eighth graders unprepared and stuff. We are going to plan our attack, just like they did in the book."

"Calvin, you reaching," Juan hesitated.

"You right I'm reaching. I'm reaching high because I'm ready to knock one of those gun slinging, handkerchief wearing blue blood suckers out. I don't want to be by myself."

"You talking about planning," Ray asked.

"And attacking," Trey continued. "You looking at these Crips like they are just eighth graders or something. True, they are eighth graders but they are also bigger and stronger. Plus, they got back up from all the Crips nationwide. How are we going to stand up to that?"

"We attack them one at a time. And we jump them. I mean, we might be short, but there is strength in our numbers, remember that. Six or seven of us ought to be able to take one of those chumps. And not all of them are bigger and taller or stronger than us. Y'all are looking at this the wrong way. You guys got to think positive thoughts. Be the train that could."

"Calvin, I'm too old for that," Franklin pouted. "And even if we did manage to beat up on one of the Crips, who's to stop the rest of them from coming after us huh? And what if they go after our moms and pops and other family members who don't have nothing to do with this? *Hello*, we are sixth graders, not eighth graders and if these guys are bold enough to shoot Sammie in the middle of the playground, what makes you think they won't bust one of us in the school hallway?"

"All the more reason to do this, man. Look, we got to start small. One victory, one fight at a time. If we are to truly run this school, not even as sixth graders but run the school period, we got to do this now."

"So we are just going to start another gang...be the Crips vs. the Bloods vs. the Sixth Graders?" Juan asked.

"No," Calvin replied confidently and with a smile on his face as he reached for another slice of pizza. I had finally finished mine...it was getting cold. "This is not a gang, this is a movement. We could be the new Black Panther Party for Self Defense...except, we can be the Sixth Grade Resistance. Better yet, why don't we become the Resistance? They were never official perse, but they were organized. We are *resisting* the gangs that are imprisoning us. The Resistance. And who said we had to be against the Bloods? The Bloods could be with us."

"But what makes you think the Bloods are going to just come over to East Middle School and come slinging with us? And what are we going to do, throw rocks while they are shooting guns?" Franklin was clearly getting frustrated with the matter.

Calvin reached for another slice of pizza, "if we do this like I know we can do this they will come. We don't need to ask them for nothing. Now if they let us drown, that is their credibility on the line, not ours. So what do y'all say, is the Resistance going to run East Middle School or what?"

"I'm with you," Arnez reached across the table and shook Calvin's hand, "I want a piece of Garfield and Freddie and if you are crazy enough to get this thing started, then I'm crazy enough to join you."

"I'm in, too," Ra-Ra finished his slice of pizza.

"Oh yeah, I'm in," Texas said.

"Of course we are in," Ray and Trey agreed.

Franklin and Darren started nodding their heads and everyone else started agreeing and supporting the idea. I was a little hesitant because I wasn't sure if I was up to being part of something revolutionary. I knew that I wanted change, but I also knew that if we or anyone one was going to enact change the first move in changing is getting started.

"So what is our first official act? Whooping Freddie or Garfield's butt?"

Calvin shook his head, "nope…on Monday, we will wear red in honor of Sammie. So call all of your friends and every sixth grader you know and tell them to wear red so that we show a united front. We'll jump Garfield and Freddie when the time was right. But if we stomp on them, we got to get ready to run because they are going to be ready for us. So are you guys ready?"

"I'm always ready," Arnez responded conceitedly.

***

I spent a majority of my Saturday on the phone calling some of the other people who I knew that were in my classes. I didn't tell them exactly what was going on, but they all went along with the lie I told about Monday being "Sixth Grade Pride Day." I don't remember when or how I came up with that lie, but I know that it worked for me. The people who I was able to get in contact with promised me that they would spread the word. Some of them were a little hesitant asking me if red was a gang color, but of course I kept up with my stream of lies and said no. I called Moesha to let her know what was up and you know she was down.

"So we are really going to do this? Wear red in broad daylight?"

"Why not?" I responded.

"I'm scared that I'm going to get shot at or killed. I'm down for this 'Sixth Grade Pride Day' but isn't there another way for us to show our pride?"

"This is the only acceptable way for us to show our pride Moesha. I am sick and tired of being oppressed. I am sick and tired of being abused. I am sick and tired of being scared and you should too. When Dr. Martin Luther King said 'free at last,' he wasn't talking about a period in the sixties. He was talking about *always* being free; free to wear what I want to wear; free to do what I want to do; free to go where I want to go."

"But we are free, we're not slaves…"

"No, we're worse than slaves. Haven't you noticed the irony of the life we are living? We are living in a modern day dictatorship; where the Crips are the Nazis and not enough people are willing or able to stand up to them. Our school is like a concentration camp where we can only hang out where we are *allowed* to hang out; play the games we are *allowed* to play. We are the Jews; only thing is that we don't wear the Star of David. We're not allowed to wear red and we have lost our right to live in a world without fear. Any moment, I could be walking down the street and get shot at because they *thought* I looked at them the wrong way; or they *thought* I was related to a Blood, or they *thought*…but you know, they don't even think. They just do.

"If I have to die, I want to die just like they did; fighting for what I believe in. And believe that there is a life better than this."

"I know…so I guess you and your boys are The Resistance, the only group of students crazy and brave enough to stand up to them."

"Yes, this is a movement. And we're not trying to kill anyone. All we want is the right to go to school, get an education, cut up a little bit without having to worry about if we are going to get shot at the end of the day. And if I am the only one who gets killed trying to make sure everyone else can enjoy the simple rights of being a kid, then I'm down for that."

"Tomorrow right?"

"Tomorrow."

I knew that Moesha was worried about me, and that maybe she wasn't old enough to comprehend or understand what she was worried about. But I knew and felt in my heart that what I was about to do was right and that no matter what happened, that at the end of the day I was going to be proud of what I was apart of. They say if you don't stand for something that you'll fall for anything. Well, if I fall, it won't be without a fight.

But he doesn't keep it buried on the inside...

If Mom and Dad knew what the real deal was, I would have never got to walk out of the house with my red on. I had on this red, black and white checked shirt that I forgot I had in the back of the closet. Under it, I had on this red and white Winston-Salem State University T-shirt with the hat to match. My grandfather got it for me last Christmas and I never got to wear it. He went to Winston-Salem State when he was younger and felt that one day, I too could become a Ram. My dad was hoping that if by chance our "Sixth Grade Pride" thing was misunderstood, that maybe someone would see my shirt and think it was the college I wanted to go to. For the first time, I felt free and I didn't have any fear.

Calvin called me to let me know that he was ready so we could go to school together. Carlton had got out of the hospital and was at home recuperating. I was going to miss watching him try to mack to all these different girls. Sometimes, I wondered if he did half of the things he said he could, but that wasn't my business. When we walked to school, we met with other students who were rocking Chicago Bulls, Atlanta Falcons, San Francisco 49ers and other professional and collegiate sports teams that had red in their logos. Some of the other students just wore regular red shirts. I didn't care, I was just happy that I wore red. Marching into the school, we looked like we were the Red Sea, and everyone parted to move out of our way.

Lester met us at our lockers and we stopped. He had the shoes Sammie wore when he got killed dangling over his shoulders. He had a picture of him and Sammie wearing red shirts dyed onto a white T-shirt. The black dickies he wore hung slightly below his waist and he was rocking some red Converses. I knew that his mother did not let him walk out of the house looking like that. In all honesty, I didn't expect him to participate in our "Sixth Grade Pride Day," but I was happy that he did. Seeing that picture of Sammie reminded me of the *real* reason we were doing this to begin with. I almost cried because I could remember Sammie getting killed all over again.

"Look at all the red," Cola interrupted our get together. She had the ugliest looking gash on her right side. She tried to style her hair so that she could cover it up but we could still see it. I looked at Calvin whose fist was balling and ready to repaint an ugly picture all over her face again. I normally don't condone violence against women, but I was willing to turn the other way while Calvin beat her tail, "y'all are some brave little boys for wearing red today."

"You brave yourself showing your face after what you did," Calvin responded coldly.

"Is there a problem?" Shanice asked as she and Allen came out of nowhere. Shanice stepped to Cola. Even though Cola had a good three inches over her, Shanice looked as if she were ready to go.

"Be nice Shanice," Allen requested.

"Oh, I'm gonna be nice..." Shanice took off her earrings and putting her hair in a pony tail. She took Allen's bandana and wrapped it around her hair. It complemented the sweater she was wearing with her pants, "see, my cousin was wrong for starting to kick her butt. But I'm not gonna be wrong for finishing it." She moved all of her rings to her left hand and Cola was looking for a way out. All of the students were looking and getting closer to see Shanice get ready to tear into Cola. Just as she got ready to get up on her, Brenda and Calvin pulled Shanice back. "Let me go!" Shanice demanded and was almost hit when Cola tried to steal a blow. Brenda pushed Shanice out of the way and grabbed Cola by the throat.

"You try to steal another blow on her and I'm gonna let her kick your butt," she let her go and turned around, "no wait a minute. *You* were the girl in on killing Carla. Yo, Shanice, come up here and get your girl."

"No Brenda, don't let them fight," Allen held Shanice behind him, "at least not here. I don't need my girl getting suspended."

"My boyfriend is going to get all of y'all! You just see! He's gonna get *all* of y'all!"

"You gonna let her walk away!" Shanice yelled.

"Look, beat her butt after school *after* you get off campus. I know where she lives anyway," Allen tried to reason with her.

"Oooh!" Shanice exhaled and went to class. Calvin followed her, surprisingly to make sure Shanice stayed out of trouble. Everyone else went to class, too.

***

Lunch time we opened up shop. Today, we were going to give the money earned to Lester so that he could help his mother pay for Sammie's funeral. I couldn't believe the funeral for that boy cost all that much, but I understood that was a lot of money for a family to come up with. A lot of students gave money just because. It was so much money that Brenda volunteered to take it and put it in her bag. I felt safe knowing the money was with her because everyone likes Brenda, and plus, no one would expect her to have the money.

Just as lunch was getting ready to end, Garfield and Freddie came to see us. I couldn't believe, no, I wasn't surprised that they showed up. I think a part of each of us wanted to kill them on sight, but we also knew they had guns and could kill us.

"What's up with all this red?" Freddie asked us, "I didn't give y'all permission to wear red."

"You didn't have to…God did," Lester boldly replied. He moved to the front of the crowd and Garfield looked away from him, "you remember him?"

Garfield started to turn and walk away and Lester followed. Naturally, we followed too because we didn't want anything to happen to our boy. Garfield turned around and he saw all this red following him and he started to run. That's when I knew that what we were doing was right and most importantly, that God *was* with us.

"I will never see my brother again because of you!" Lester ran faster than I ever thought he could run. He caught up with Garfield and Garfield turned around and stopped. He went for his piece and Lester boldly walked up closer to him, "go ahead and kill me because then I can play with my brother in heaven. But do know that you can't kill all of us. And when those bullets run out, we're gonna get you sucka!"

Garfield pointed the gun and aimed it at Lester's face.

"Go ahead! Pull the trigger!" Lester dared him.

Garfield shook his head and Freddie grabbed the gun from him. They turned and walked away until they were off campus. Lester wanted to, but he didn't follow. I was scared, but at the same time, I was ready for him to pull the trigger. I don't know why, but my adrenaline was rushing and was ready for whatever was going to come my way. I felt like I was living in the modern day civil rights standoff. Far from nonviolent, but not close enough to the militant either.

***

After school, we met on the black ground to play basketball, or so it appeared. Yeah, we dribbled the ball, did some jump shots and some lay ups. What we were really up to was more serious. We were plotting to take over the school. Not to have recess all the time, but so that we can have fun going to school, not this modern day concentration camp we found ourselves in. We wanted to learn and feel free to learn. This was 1994, not 1954, and too many people gave their lives so that we could have this thing called freedom. But there was one thing standing in our way.

"Mama said knock you out!" Juan shouted at the top of his lungs.

"We are not going to have a theme song Juan," I was clearly agitated.

"Why not? Every great fighter has a theme song."

"That's only in movies Juan," Arnez chastised, "besides, who is going to bring a boom box to the playground anyway. That would be too loud and we need the element of surprise on our side."

"Well I'm gonna knock you out!"

"Juan, quit playing and be serious," Calvin replied, "if we are going to take over the school, everyone needs to stick to the plan. The plan was that we attack Tony and Cedric first.

Garfield never comes to school on Thursdays and Freddie will be too busy trying to get up on Clarice."

"Clarice? That chick that Carlton was trying to feel on?" Ray asked.

"Yeah, but that's beside the point," Arnez got everyone back on subject, "the point is, we need to attack when we know we can control the situation. I say the best time is when they try to sneak off for their smoke break."

"It's gonna be a smoke break alright, 'cause I'm a smoke them," Cisco pulled out a gun from him bag. We rushed in to see whether or not it was real.

"Are you crazy?" Calvin yelled, "Are you trying to get us expelled?"

"No, I want to smoke 'em."

"There will be no guns!" Lester said sternly. "You hear me man! No guns!"

"Aight calm down," Cisco put the gun away. Texas and Trey kept playing with Darren, trying to double team him, "but we need a weapon. They got guns, so what are we gonna use?"

"I like to throw rocks," Calvin threw in, "but whatever weapons we do use, we got to make sure it's not something illegal. We can't come empty handed."

"The jump rope," I spoke as if I had an epiphany.

"Jump rope?" Arnez questioned.

"Yeah, a jump rope, a basketball and yes, even some rocks. These are things that can be found on the playground. The rocks are small enough to sneak on campus and the jump rope is fast and quick like a whip."

"And what are we gonna do with the basketball?"

"Roll the ball like a bowling ball so that one of them trips."

"Oh I get it," Juan jumped in, "I like that idea."

"Yeah, me too," Arnez said.

We rejoined the game and finished playing. At the same time we discussed other ideas for our takeover. I was excited about how things were going to go down. I was nervous too because I was never really the fighting type, but I was ready for this.

United we stood...

The first day of attack was perfect. We came to school just like the Black Panthers in all black. The modern day resistance to the black Nazis was in full affect. Calvin came out of the bathroom donning his red Chicago Bulls jersey and Juan followed suit in a red jumpsuit. Some students took notice as more of us where wearing red and boldly. I didn't look so bad myself. I had on a red and black checkered button up shirt with red and black doo-rags to match. The white kids were like "it's about time" and they too started putting on their red shirts. I was glad they were down with the movement, but they had no clue what we were about to get into.

"Look at this," Cedric skipped class to come to our lunch period, "they wearing red."

"Got to give it them," Tony walked up to Calvin, "these l'il dudes bold! They know it's on now!"

Calvin had the biggest grin I'd ever seen plastered on his face. He started to walk toward Cedric and Tony and I followed suit. Pretty soon, Juan, Ray, Trey, Darren and Lester were right behind us.

"So what is this, the l'il Blood convention? What y'all wearing red for?" Tony asked. He turned his head and his dreads whispered as he turned around to see if anyone else was behind him. Some of the white students were standing on the side lines just waiting on for something to happen. Truthfully, I think we should have put them in the front so that if anything went down, they could get they butt beat first. Just playing, they were fine where they were at, which was out of the damn way.

"We got to put these l'il punks in they place. They must think they Kriss Kross and gonna make us jump."

"Naw, they gonna be totally crossed out of the map when we are done with them."

"Y'all talk a lot of junk for some fools that's about to get wrecked," Calvin said boldly.

"Wrecked? Negro please, the only thing that is going to get wrecked is your face." Tony said.

"Yo, I'm tired of this l'il rug rat. I'm about to smash him."

"Ain't nothing but space and opportunity, brother." Calvin replied. Tony stepped to Calvin and Calvin pushed him back.

"Man, he pushes like a l'il girl." Tony said, "feel this."

Tony and Cedric started play pushing each other and laughing. Then Tony got serious and swung at Calvin. Calvin ducked and out of nowhere, he raised his left fist and socked Tony in the jaw.

"Aw, hell naw, I'm gonna get this l'il nigga!" Tony swore as he swung at Calvin and missed.

Calvin punched Cedric and Tony. Darren followed suit swinging at both of them. Trey and Ray pushed Cedric away from Tony and started punching at him as well. The white students started moving toward the middle of the crowd, separating Cedric and Tony even further. I could see Juan on top of Cedric getting mad blows to his face. I knew the boy had it in him. Calvin started running and Tony followed him. I was so amazed at Cedric getting his butt whooped that I almost forgot my role. I ran after them in hopes that Calvin wouldn't get cornered by himself.

"Martin! Where the hell you at?" Calvin yelled as he ended up outside of the building.

"Behind you!" I yelled.

I had started gaining on Tony and he turned around and started running toward me.

"You want some of this!" Tony barked at me.

"What's up man?" I meant to say no, but I already knew that I was going to get my licks in. "Calvin, turn around!"

"Oh, what, y'all gonna try to jump me now?"

"I don't need to jump you," I balled my fist. I put them to my waist quickly to see if my club was still at my side.

Tony tackled me and to my surprise, I got in two licks on his face. He started delivering body blows and I could see Calvin standing over him. I moved my head as Calvin kicked him one time. Tony jumped up and he turned to face Calvin.

"You mother…" before he could finish I quickly drew my billy club and swung at his back. He turned to face me and Calvin grabbed his locks and I swung on his face again. Out of nowhere, Arnez and Ra-Ra start tackling him and then they get up and start stomping on him. Texas was pulling Calvin away from under Tony so that he wouldn't get any of the kicks. Calvin drew his knife and started to run toward the crowd. Texas caught up with him and got in front of him.

"Not today man, save it for Garfield."

Calvin ran toward the crowd and started to get some licks in on Tony. I could see Juan and Darren running toward us. Juan's shirt was torn off of him. I could see the teachers and the police running toward the crowd and chaos erupting.

"Break!" Calvin yelled and everyone started running in different directions. We took our red shirts off and we started to enter the school in different directions. We put on our black shirts and got our books so that we could go to class. Allen met up with us and took all of our red shirts and he and Second took our clothes to some guy they knew off campus.

Lunch time was over and we all went to class as if nothing happened. I was nervous because I was waiting on the principal to call us one by one to go to his office as if we had been caught, but that wasn't the case at all. The rest of the day we were able to finish school and we didn't even see Cedric or Tony again. When school got out, we all went to Darren's house to celebrate. Darren's aunt was home, but she was cool with all of us hanging out in front of her house. Lester looked at Elkhart like he was waiting on Sammie to run from the school and start looking for him.

"Let's go to the school," Calvin suggested.

"I don't want to go," Lester said as if he were going to start crying.

"Naw, we are going to have to go back to that place eventually. We all will. Let's just go now," Calvin commanded.

We started walking to the school and Lester started sobbing. We knew it was going to be hard but we finally stood at the place where Sammie lost his life. We said a prayer and then we looked into the sky. We were hoping that Sammie was looking down on us, smiling, and maybe, just maybe, he had a candy bar in his hand.

For the right to be what we wanted...

Calvin, Lester and the Twins skipped school today. Juan was about an hour late and Darren left early. As trifling as this sounds, this was all part of the plan so that everyone wouldn't catch on or care that we jumped Tony and Cedric. So it was me and the girls all day.

"So what do, we get to do?" Shanice asked me. "I want to whoop some butt too."

"Girl be quiet," Lisa jumped in, "always trying to fight somebody."

"Well that's better than traveling the world and trying to get with every man I see."

"What are you trying to say?" Moesha got defensive. I did too and I looked at her and wondered who all had been with her. Renee and Pamela seen me look at her and started laughing. All of a sudden, I felt a little insecure because I hadn't been with anyone and Moesha may have been with more people than I cared to count. But those are just rumors, and if that were true, that wouldn't have nothing to do with me.

"But let me see Cola walk around here once and it's on!" Shanice was getting 'bout it.

"You still trying to fight that girl?" Angela asked as she was trying to put some more gloss on her protruding lips.

"It's not going to be a fight, I'm a beat her down. She's just lucky that Brenda jumped in when she did. And then Allen has been all up on me lately."

I didn't want to hear about Allen kicking it with Shanice. Even though I got a girl, a part of me wanted to be with Shanice. I didn't think I would be able to get with her like that, but the thought was always there. I felt tortured as I listed to Shanice talk about Allen this, Allen that. I was so tired of hearing about Allen I was starting to hate on him. Clarice and Cola walked past and Lisa and Renee quickly began to hold Shanice back.

"I wish that girl *would* jump on me," Cola started to get loud and showing off in front of her friend.

"Cola, you are too big and too old to be worried about these little girls," Clarice scolded her.

"If she is too old for little girls then why is she rolling her eyes at me? Why she got something smart to say when she sees *me*?" Shanice yelled.

"Girl, ain't nobody worried about you," Cola said.

"You think because you killed Carla that I should be scared of you?" Shanice challenged, breaking away from Lisa.

Cola stopped and turned around. Her bag dropped. Clarice went to hold her back but Cola jerked away. "I'm getting sick and tired of you saying that. I didn't have nothing to do with Carla getting killed. She was at the wrong place, at the wrong time, with the wrong crew."

"You were supposed to be her girl!"

"I don't roll with Bloods."

"Whatever, you was kicking it with Carla every chance you got. You was just mad that you weren't as beautiful and as sophisticated as she was."

"Oh my God she said *sophisticated*," Cola repeated with a neck roll, "little girl probably don't know what *sophisticated* means!"

"You don't look like you know what it means."

All of the girls started rolling. Cola walked to Shanice and Shanice clocked her in the jaw. Shanice followed with a right to her eye. Clarice started to jump in and all the girls got up on her. Clarice pulled Cola away as she starts calling her all kinds of B's and hoes.

"I told that girl not to roll up on me. I fight like I could be Ali's daughter," Shanice rearranged her hair so that the braids flow around her bandana. Shanice threw some more fake punches pretending like she was still beating on Cola, "now I can look pretty again."

"Girl you are a mess," Lisa adds.

"No, she is a mess," Shanice replied as she looked at her hands. She scrunched up face and looked as if she was disgusted again, "I broke my nail! I'm a beat that…"

"Girl stop that, you just won the fight," Angela scolded.

"You didn't know! I'm *always* ready to fight."

***

After school I opened up shop. Normally, I don't sell any candy after school, but today isn't an average day. As I worked my way through the crowds of people who have complained about not finding me this morning. I saw Freddie rushing to get through the crowd. Second and Brenda were given the day off so that it would appear as if I were alone. I tried to end my candy sells but a Negro like me was in high demand. I couldn't disappoint my customers.

"Yo! Martin! Let me get at you," Freddie yelled as he was trying to get through the crowd. I saw him, but I finished working on my sales. "Break away fool! Quit acting like a punk!"

I looked at him but kept selling my candy. Everyone just started moving closer to me and then moving away. Truth was, I wasn't in high demand like that. I got some of the other sixth graders just to walk back and forth through the crowd pretending to be salespeople or new customers. I was a little nervous, but all I had to do was just stick with the plan.

"You thought you was cool trying to jump on my boys. Here I am by myself man, me and you!"

Since when did Crips fight someone one on one? I wasn't even gonna let that faze me. I looked to my left and I could see Calvin standing on a car that was creeping through the parking lot. I didn't know who was driving but as he got closer, the crowd of people moved out of the way. I ducked down and I slipped through the crowd of people trying to get away. I was so caught up in the moment that I didn't see Freddie standing in front of me and I walked into him. I looked up and he looked down at me. I seen the rock coming and I ducked. The rock sounded like a whistle as it danced across Freddie's face. I looked back up and I could see two more rocks land on Freddie's head. Perfect! Freddie looked back at Calvin, who promptly threw him the bird. Freddie started to run after Calvin and I started to run after him. I was feeling lucky so I tried to kick his ankle so that he could fall, but instead, he turned around and my foot landed on his shin. Freddie tackled me like a defensive lineman on a quarterback. I immediately tried to get some blows in on his face, and I got a good shot at his nose.

"You little…" I tried to kick him in his balls or something because Freddie was even bigger than I had thought. He must have grown a little since I saw him last. Freddie punched me in the jaw, but that wasn't what hurt. Texas and Cisco were stomping on Freddie and some of those feet landed on me. I could feel Freddie being rolled over and he was trying to roll me on top of him to shield him from the onslaught of sixth graders handling their business. I could feel some hands pulling me up.

"Don't want you to get none of what he is getting!" I looked up and I could see Bernie and Eric pulling me away from the crowd. I was shocked because I didn't expect any seventh graders to be trying to help out at all, other than Second and Allen.

"Y'all are not playing with them eighth graders!" Eric was excited, "y'all are nasty with y'alls."

"Well…they shouldn't have killed Sammie."

I watched Freddie try to get out of the crowd and everyone kept stomping on him. I felt a little sorry for him because if I was still under there, I would be getting whooped and I probably would be in pain right about now. However, I had no remorse because he was part of the problem. He was part of the reason why no one can have fun in this city. He was the reason that Garfield killed Sammie. So my hurt and sympathy was replaced with a cold hearted feeling of hatred. I called for my boys to leave and as they broke away, I saw more and more seventh graders that were in on the action than I had anticipated. This was going a little better than we had planned it. I only wished that Garfield would have been here because he could have gotten his too. Freddie lay there, limping and crying. His face was swollen and there was blood all over his clothes. He looked like a few bullets had run through him. He was yelling in pain and trying to call out for his boys but no one was there to save him. But then again, no one was there to save his victims either. Karma was something wasn't it?

Even if that means becoming the prey...

My dad had questioned me about the wave of violence that he heard about at East Middle School. I guess word of our revolt was traveling around the metropolitan area quicker than I thought. So I did the one thing I *knew* that I knew better not to do. I lied. Not to protect myself, but to keep him and Mom from worrying about me. I know they don't think I'm innocent, but I can't concentrate on what I need to do if they are worrying about me.

"So I don't need to remove you from that school? You can always be home schooled," Dad suggested.

"No, I'm going to be okay."

"You say that as if you are part of the problem and not part of the solution."

"I'm not part of the problem. I want to be part of the solution."

"You're gonna be part of the solution with a bullet in your butt."

I shook my head. I shouldn't have done that but his worrying was starting to wear on me. He always swore that when I had my own kids I would appreciate what he was doing for my brother and I. I wanted to exhale but I kept it to myself. I decided at the last minute that I was going to change clothes. I knew that today would be the day that we would get our revenge on Garfield, possibly kill him and for that I was scared. I had always been ready to fight and even ready to die, but now that was becoming a reality, I didn't know how sure I was that I was ready to do either. I just knew that this battle and our pending freedom were worth fighting for. I wore these dark blue jeans with a red and blue Karl Kani shirt that I haven't worn in a while. I was against wearing something blue but today I decided that I didn't want to stand out in the crowd. I could have worn my orange and green CrossColour outfit that I had but I decided against that too. I just wanted to go to school and not worry too much about what was or could or may happen to me.

My dad had called Calvin's parents and had offered to drive us to school. I wasn't feeling that move too much because if anything was going to happen, I wanted it to happen the way it was *supposed* to happen.

"Leave the candy here. We need to talk about the few hundred dollars that have *disappeared* in the last few days. I want to know what you bought. But I'm going to give you the whole day to decide if you are going to lie to me or tell me the truth. Then your mother and I will decide whether or not you will continue your studies at East."

He looked at me like he knew what had been going down all along. But if he did, he would understand *why* I'm doing what I'm doing. If anything, I'm like his father. I'm standing up for what I believe in and what I feel is right. I thought that that was what they had always wanted me to do. Carlton and Calvin knocked on the door a few minutes later and we were off to school. I was happy to see that Carlton was doing okay and was well. He wasn't the fun loving older brother whom we've come to know. He seemed more reserved and somewhat tense. I guess I would feel that way too if today was my first day of school and I knew that a war was going on. As we got into the car, a part of me wanted to ask Dad to cover our license plate, as I began to fear the possibility that the Crips could have been following us. Calvin looked as if he was up to something mischievous, which wouldn't surprise me one bit, but I knew that he wouldn't try anything in front of my father. The ride was fairly quite except for Dad teaching Marcus how to drive...sort of. He let him turn the steering wheel. I remembered when I used to do that and part of me wished that I was Marcus' age again.

We got to the school and everything looked quiet. As if Freddie getting jumped on yesterday didn't happen. Dad dropped us off and we walked into the building to our class. I went to my locker to change books and to get some supplies and to my surprise no one came up to me and asked me for any candy. Then the thought occurred to me that everyone's parents knew about what was going on and that my father wasn't the only one issuing talks between last night and this morning. It was only at lunch time when someone mentions what was going on.

"We still up for whooping Garfield's butt if we can catch him aren't we?" Trey asked.

"I don't think Garfield is going to show up," Juan answered, "so many people know about what is going on and us fighting them like that and people in the neighborhoods are talking about how Garfield killed Sammie in front of all us until I don't know what to think."

"I'm surprised the police haven't arrested him yet," Ray jumped in.

"We need to hope that the police don't arrest us," Darren replied, "you know we can go to jail for this?"

"I'm ready to go to jail," Calvin said as he got up. Cisco, Texas, Ra-Ra and Arnez come to sit at our table, too.

"I'm not going to jail," Ra-Ra commented, "I'm too pretty to be in jail, I'll probably do some community service."

"Whatever, holmes," Arnez said. "If I go to jail, you're coming with me."

"You'd snitch on me?"

"We could run the jail."

"Yeah right! Those people in there are bigger than Garfield and them."

We ate our food and continued to talk. We watched the girls play and gossip and laugh as if nothing happened. And maybe that was what we should be doing. Playing it off like nothing happened...that was plan until Bernie and Second showed up.

"You guys are some legends," Bernie commented, "some soon to be dead legends, but some legends nevertheless."

"What are you talking about?" I asked.

"Martin, don't act like you don't know. Everyone one in Denver knows about how y'all jumped on Freddie after school yesterday. I wasn't home for ten minutes before my people's phone was blowing up with some of my cousins and other friends asking about what went down. Everyone's been talking about it. My grandma came to see me yesterday to make sure I was okay."

"Are you serious?" Lester asked.

"Yeah man, y'all in some serious stuff," Second added. "I know I'm bold but I'm not *that* bold. Folks are excited, scared, happy, angry and confused all at the same time."

"My mom's talked to me before I left for school this morning," Juan said, "*don't get involved in that mess they got going up there hermano. I want you to come home later on today.*"

We laughed at Juan's imitation of his mother. We needed that because things were just too serious and in some ways, we had gone back to where things were before with everyone acting scared and not knowing what they could or couldn't do. This was not what we were fighting for.

"I didn't see too many of them eighth graders up here this morning. They must be plotting on y'all." Bernie said.

"Don't act like some of y'all weren't getting licks in," Calvin defended us. "I seen Christian and DeVante getting some stomps in too."

"I had nothing to do with that."

"You do now, because if they come after us, they are going to come after you guys too. Bullets don't have eyes son."

"Son! Boy, I'm old enough to be your daddy!"

"But you're not."

We started laughing again. I looked around and I didn't see DeVante or Christian anywhere. That could be because Bernie and Second were skipping class. When we got tired of sitting in the cafeteria, we all went outside to play basketball. I didn't get to play because no one picked me for there team so I just looked out for any suspicious activity. I was nervous about whether or not they were just going to roll up on the playground and start shooting at us. I was ready to run if they did. We did see Tony and Cedric sneaking off for their smoke break. They looked at us and grinned and went on their way. We decided not to be bothered with them because we were having fun and we wanted to keep it that way.

***

School got out and the crew was at the locker. Folks had come by to ask if we had candy and only Darren had a candy bag. He sold all of his candy in three minutes. We were getting ready to walk home when Eric and DeVante came running our way.

"They here!"

"Garfield's here," Calvin got excited, "oh, it's on now!"

"No, you don't understand. They are looking for all of you. You guys need to run. Look, I'll show y'all where they are at."

We followed Eric and DeVante to the seventh grade wing, which allowed us to see the front of the school. Garfield and some people we never seen before were walking around and searching through cars and stuff.

"Where these little bad kids at! They want to fight, we can fight!" Garfield was heard yelling.

There was no way we were going to able to take on Garfield and the crew he bought with him. They looked like an army. Maybe we should not have jumped Freddie like we did… naw, this was what it was going to come down to.

"Where they at now! I killed that little bastard two weeks ago and I'll kill all of them this week! Don't make no difference to me!"

We all looked at each other.

"Y'all got to split up because if y'all are in a group, they will surround you guys and then kill all of you together. But if y'all leave separately and go in different directions, you will have a better chance of surviving. They are looking for a group of you. We'll hold them off for as long as we can but we're not going to promise that they still won't come after you," Christian offered.

We gave everyone in our group pound and we started to leave the school in separate directions. As we were leaving, we ran into the Hispanic guys.

"They shot at Ra-Ra!" Arnez yelled. "I don't know if he made it or not. They caught us as we were getting ready to cross Chambers into that apartment complex by Hinkley."

"We got to split up," I told them and pretty soon, we all were on our way. We ran through Elkhart and some of the guys thought they could catch the bus with them so they stayed at the school. Texas and I decided that we were going to take our chances and run through the streets. We ran down this one street, forgot the name of it but we kept running and no looking back. We could hear a car drive by the next street over and loud gangsta rap being played from it. Texas and I kept running until we got to 6th Avenue. We could still hear the car and we didn't know whether or not they had found us so we kept running. Against our better judgment, we ran out into the busy street. We got to the middle lane where people turn into the shopping center. We heard bullets and felt them whizzing by us. I turned around for one minute and I could see that the Crips were shooting at us. That was all I needed for me to just take that leap of faith and run across the street and roll down the hill in the shopping center. It was a bumpy ride but when it was over, I looked up and seen that Texas was still running in front of the shopping center. I decided to take the longer route and go behind the center. Texas didn't know where I lived and I was worried about him because I didn't know if Calvin had made it home or not. When I came from around the shopping center, I could see them in the parking lot. I just took my chances and ran up to the gates and into the apartment complex. I could see Texas walking to my building so I followed suite.

"Texas!" I shouted. He turned around and smiled at me. He stopped so I could catch up to him, "Garfield knows where I live."

"Where are we gonna go?"

"We're better off at my crib than we are at Calvin's. Besides, my father will be home soon and I doubt he'd put up with Garfield coming to the house like that."

We walked to my apartment and to my surprise the television had been left on. I called for Dad but he didn't answer. I checked all the rooms in the house to make sure that no one else was in the house and when all was squared away I came back into the living room with Texas. He exhaled loudly. "That was close."

"Yeah, it was," I grabbed the remote and I turned on the television. I couldn't remember if Bill Bellamy was going to be on MTV or not so I just turned to the channel anyway hoping some good music would come on, "you want some KoolAid?"

"What kind you got?"

"Red."

"Red is tight."

I poured Texas and myself a drink in some plastic cups in the kitchen. I gave Texas his cup and he downed his in one second. He looked at me and cracked a grin.

"That's what I call KoolAid," he helped himself to some water, "mi abuela puts limes and some kind of tart salt in hers, but it's good nevertheless."

"I got to try that sometime."

There was a loud booming at the door. I was scared because I knew that wasn't my father and my mother wasn't due home until later on tonight. I knew it was Garfield, but I wasn't about to open the door. I opened the drawer and reached for a knife. Texas pulled out a blade from his waistband. I went to the door, hoping that whoever it was that was knocking on the door didn't have gun on the other end. When I looked through the peephole, all I saw was a finger print and ran into the room. Texas came in after me and I crept my way to the window. I could see some of Garfield's boys outside walking around the pool. I moved away from the window and I walked over to where my bed was and reached under it for a bat.

"Get in the closet!" I commanded.

"Naw, if you out here, I need to be out here. I can't let them get at you in your house by yourself. We are in this together!"

The booming stopped and was replaced with someone trying to key their way into the apartment. I quickly ran out of the room and put the top latch on the door. Wasn't going to do us a lot of good but I figured it would buy us some time to come up with a plan.

"You stab at the bottom and I'll swing the bat from the top. We know what they got but they don't know what we got."

Texas and I moved to the door. Texas looked out the peep hole and he stood behind me while I was crouching ready for action. My heart was beating real fast, almost to the rhythm of an African drum beat. Pretty soon the door knob kept jingling. I looked at Texas and Texas looked at me, he ran into my room and I ran into the living room. I heard a gun shot go off and I ran into the kitchen. I took a quick look out the window and I could see their car speed off blasting their music. I went back to the door and I looked at the peep hole. I could see the neighbor's door and for a minute I felt safe. I walked back to my room and I could see Texas peeping out the window. I walked into my parent's room and snuck a look out of their window and I could see that they were indeed gone. The phone rang and I picked it up from my parents' room.

"Little residence," I said trying to conceal my nervousness.

"You aight in there?" Calvin half yelled in my ear.

"Yeah man, we're cool. I'm glad to know you made it home okay."

"We saw you and Texas running across the street. You almost got hit."

"Where were you?"

"Dad came to pick us up. We drove by your place and we could see Garfield and his crew staking out your apartment. Dad called the cops after he made sure Carlton, Shanice and Ra-Ra got in the house okay."

"Ra-Ra's okay?"

"Yeah man, he got grazed a little bit, but nothing he would have to go to the hospital for. He's lucky."

"We're lucky, too."

"Hey, we are gonna come and get you and Texas and you guys can hang out at our crib."

"Thanks man."

We hung up the phone and I walked to the door. I opened it to see if any kind of damage was done to the outside door. The knob looked scratched a little but other than that, it was cool. I did not feel too safe with them guys at the door like that. I was even more worried about Garfield trying to get at my mom's or something. Then I felt peace. I had seen Carlton, Calvin, Shanice and Ra-Ra coming up the stairs as Texas and I were getting ready to leave. As I was locking the door, I could see where they had shot into the neighbor's apartment by mistake. I realized then that my life was precious and not to be tampered with by anyone. Then this feeling came over me that made me feel as if I were being carried off into a better place. I thanked God for allowing me to survive this wild and crazy afternoon.

And always being the haunted...

The teachers had the day off and so did we. I was glad because all this fighting and getting shot at and other violence was wearing on my nerves. My parents took it easy on me last night and I was able to avoid talking about getting shot at and Texas being at the house. My dad and I agreed that it was best not to tell my mother until I figured out exactly what I got myself into. Plus, we didn't want her worrying at the shop and my dad didn't think that Garfield would do anything to harm my mother, especially since his mother was at the shop all the time. It must have been hard for Garfield's mother to come into the shop knowing that her son was the biggest monster in Denver and I know she was hearing the stuff that was going down if my father had heard it. I really felt sorry for her because I knew and felt that she did not raise her son to be the way he was.

I planned on staying home, getting some much needed rest and perhaps rethinking the selection of candy that I was selling. I was hoping that when all this was over with that my father would still allow me to sell candy. I enjoyed having my business and making my own money. I don't have to ask for money every time *I* want something. Only thing I don't like was carrying around all this cash. But the weekly trips to the bank were hot, too. The account was getting bigger and bigger which means I can buy more when I wanted to. My boys are spending their money on new gear or toys and stuff like that. Juan was sporting the new Mahmoud Abdul-Rauf

Denver Nuggets jersey. I was surprised because he swore up and down with he's an Orlando Magic fan. Lester used most of his money to help pay for Sammie's funeral. I don't know what Calvin spent his money on. I really didn't keep up with what my boys were spending their money on, I was watching where my money was going. It's not like we made a million dollars but what we had was respectable. My train of thought was lost when the phone rang.

"Little residence," I responded.

"Sup fool!" Calvin was playing on the phone.

"Just hanging out. Thinking about a lot of things."

"Man, I want to finish this."

"Finish what?"

"Whooping Garfield's butt! I wish I could put a bullet in his butt."

"Texas and I almost got killed yesterday crossing the street. I don't know what is going on, this is crazy!"

"It's gonna be crazy. As long as we are fighting it's gonna be crazy. But the important thing is that we are fighting for what is right. That's all that matters."

"But there's got to be more to it than that."

"It is…when this is over, we will have our childhood, or what's left of it. Look at it this way, when Casey and Marcus get to be our age, they won't go through all of the BS we are going through. We're doing this for them."

"You really see it that way?"

"Of course. I always saw it that way. I may not act like it, but I'm a big brother, too. I'm going to look out for my family and do what is best for them."

"Me too."

"Is your dad going to let you hang out with us today? I promise to stay out of trouble."

"He didn't say I couldn't leave, and what about Marcus?"

"Just bring him to our house. Our mom is home and she's not going to mind."

"Are you sure about that?"

"Man, come on!"

"Aight, give me five minutes."

I hung up the phone and I went into our room. Marcus was coloring in a book in his pajamas. I went into our closet and try to find something for him to wear.

"Can we go outside and play?"

"Yep little man. We'll get to play in a minute. I'm taking you to Casey's but you got to be dressed first."

Surprisingly, I was able to get Marcus to change with no problems. I changed into a matching outfit…something I normally don't do but I appreciate the fact that I have a brother. I never knew how much I would love and appreciate the boy until Sammie go killed. Lester used to love walking to Elkhart to pick Sammie up, now he can't stand to walk past the school. Before we left, I made sure to grab a baseball bat, just in case I needed it. I held Marcus' hand tightly as I locked the door. We walked down the stairs and heading to Calvin's. Calvin's mother was outside in the car where she was getting Casey situated.

"Martin, did you leave your parents a note letting them know you were going out?"

"I forgot."

"Go back and write that note so they don't be worried about you. I'll call your mother at the shop okay?"

"Thank you."

I ran back to the house and I quickly wrote my parents a note. I locked the door again and I flew down the stairs back to Calvin's where I seen their mother take off with Marcus and Casey in tow. Calvin and Carlton were outside, playing catch. Carlton looked a lot better than he did yesterday. We greeted and pretty soon, I was in on the game of catch too.

"Who was the girl you were talking to yesterday?" Calvin asked. I was surprised that he would be interested in his brother's exploits.

"Kimberly," Carlton threw the ball at me, "I don't think I'm going to mess with her. I heard she likes them bad boys and I'm trying to stay away from that."

"Yeah, stay away from the bad girls."

Carlton caught the ball and he started walking toward the store. Calvin and I followed and pretty soon, we were 6th Avenue again. I was surprised that it was not as busy as it was. After safely walking across the street, we walked toward the school. I felt like I had left my backpack and my bag of candy as we got closer to the school. I was surprised to see a large group of sixth and seventh graders were playing dodge ball in broad daylight. I was madder that no one called and asked if I wanted to play. Punks! I sat in the stands and watched a mixture of students play and have fun. Everyone was laughing and having fun and what have you. In no time, Carlton was really back to his old self, macking to some chick that went to Hinkley…at least I think she went to Hinkley.

Allen, Second and some of Allen's boys came to watch the game. I hadn't seen Allen since everything was on a popping with Garfield and stuff. Allen looked me in the eye and cracked a smile.

"Let me find out it's the sixth graders who run things around here." Allen embraced us and sat down. "If I had known that y'all got down like that then I would have put y'all on way before now."

"It's not like that Allen. We're just fed up that's all. Fed up and we want to bring Sammie back," I had gotten frustrated.

"You know all of this is not going to bring Sammie back."

"I know, but I want a life back. A good, fun, life back. I deserve that...and so does everyone else."

"I agree."

We could hear loud music pull up in the playground getting ready to spoil the mood. Garfield, Cedric, Tony and some other cat they had with them got out of the car and walked onto the play ground. I reached for my bat to make sure I still had it with me. Everyone else stopped playing what they were playing and started to get their stuff. Next thing I know, there were a large assortment of bats and knives and other weapons being assembled. I just knew that this would be the start of World War III.

"You can't leave my girls alone can you?" Garfield walked up on Carlton.

"What are you talking about?" the girl asked. "I am not your girl. And you are not that big anyway."

All the girls in the playground were rolling and the guys were ooing and ahhing at the hidden meaning behind the girl's words.

"Why is it every time you step up here you got to have your crew with you, like you can't handle business by yourself?" Allen stepped to him.

"Negro please, you know you do the same thing."

"You see any other Bloods up here? And don't even look at my boy like that because he don't get down like that. If he was then I'd claim it, he'd claim it."

"What you trying to say?"

"That I could whoop your butt one on one, in front of your boys and all these people here but you can't fight a fair fight."

"Is that right?"

"That's right. Now you come to step up to your boy over here and you bring your people up here. You got your guns and your connections and all this other stuff. This dude don't have nobody over here that got his back but some kids. Some kids that have whooped your crew's tail nevertheless but these are some kids! You are sixteen, seventeen years old or something like that, almost grown and you harassing and messing around with some *kids*? I can't even respect you man."

Garfield looked at his crew and he cocked a grin, "aight, I'll play your game. I'll whoop that little scrub's butt and afterwards, I can kick yours, too."

"We'll see," Allen replied.

Carlton got up as people started surrounding him. I couldn't believe that he was going to get into a fight so soon after getting well, but sometimes it happens like that.

"If I had known I was going to be in a boxing match, I would have brought my gloves," Carlton remarked.

"Shut up," Garfield stole him and Carlton stumbled back. Calvin wanted to jump in it but Second was holding him back.

"Let your brother whoop his butt!"

Calvin rolled his eyes at Second but he stood to the side and watched. Carlton and Garfield were shoulder to shoulder and Garfield pushed him back. Garfield got two blows off of Carlton's face and started to tackle him but Carlton caught him and pushed him off. Carlton got a blow off of Garfield's face and the two of them started dancing around like real boxers. Carlton started throwing some jabs, some right and left hooks. Cedric and Tony wasn't liking this at all because after awhile, things weren't looking good for Garfield. Carlton had been practicing on his swings and his boxing game for a few years now and after a while, this lover boy was starting to turn into a young Evander Holyfield in front of our eyes. Don't get me wrong, Garfield was holding his own in there but Carlton was whooping that ass! I know that Garfield was getting mad and not able to concentrate because he was out of his element. The fact that everyone was cheering Carlton on wasn't helping matters either. Finally, Carlton knocked Garfield flat on his back with a combo and the crowd started cheering him. Garfield quickly got on his feet and wanted to reach for his piece, but he forgot that he handed to Tony. When Tony tried to hand it to him, Allen was quick on the draw.

"We done had us a nice clean fight...don't make me mess it up. I'm quicker on my aim than Carlton is with his fist," Allen managed to put one on Tony's head and the other aimed at Cedric's chest.

Garfield scratched his neck, looked around and then signaled for his boys to follow him. Everyone on the playground was cheering and celebrating Carlton's win. Hell, I was, too. I couldn't believe he won like that, but I was happy all the same.

"We won!" Lester and Darren started chanting. I couldn't believe it but now that Garfield has gotten his butt whooped publicly, we did win. Of course, we had some outside help here and there, but *we* won. In some ways it felt good to beat Garfield on the very field that he took Sammie's life. I felt like Sammie had been avenged, somewhat. Truth was Allen was right, Carlton winning, us winning, did not bring Sammie back. But what it did do was give us a sense of hope and pride to know that we fought hard for the freedom that we were about to enjoy. We earned that freedom.

Soon the day will pass...

This was just like I remembered in *Schindler's List*. Students were lined up one after another heading into the journey unknown. The Aurora Police Department looked like the army with their protective gear. The school was barricaded like it was Fort Knox. Only school busses were allowed to arrive on the school property. Parents were informed to drop their children off at several check stations where our bags were searched before we're allowed on school property. All of my boys and I had our bags of candy taken away. We were giving a warning to end our business on campus or face suspension.

Once we made it to the inside of the school, we had to separate into the halls where our homerooms were located. Our teachers were waiting on us at the entrance of the hall. Again, we had to check in with some teachers, who escorted us to our homerooms, one line at a time. Once we got to our homeroom, we had assigned seats, which were lined up alphabetical order. In the back of our classroom, we had a police officer sitting down. He was trying to look mean as hell but something told me he was scared of us. It took an hour before they started class. Our principal came on the intercom.

"Look, I don't want to have to do this everyday, but I can and I will! The war is over and anyone participating in violent activities will be expelled for the rest of the year, no questions asked. There is no reason why our school shouldn't be safe for students to come here and get an education. I hope that is what you guys have come here for. For the rest of the day and possibly the rest of this week, everyone will be under strict observation so it will be to your best benefit to behave yourselves while you are on campus. I'm going to go on with a reminder of a few school rules and then I am going to let the teachers get on with their classes:

"For starters, the obvious is no fighting or other forms of violent behavior. Any student or students who break this rule face automatic expulsion.

"Secondly, there will be no weapons brought on campus and no educational instrument shall be used as a weapon. Any student or students who break this rule will face automatic expulsion.

"Next, if you are a member of a gang, then you are not a student of East Middle School. As of this moment, all gang members posing as students will be arrested for trespassing and all students that participate in gang activity are expelled. Throughout the day we will be calling parents or other legal guardians to pick you up. You can do that gangster stuff off campus but you will not be doing it at East.

"Anyone caught dealing drugs, be they legal or illegal will be face automatic expulsion.

"Only employees of the school and select non-profit organizations are allowed to sell items on campus. Anyone who is a member of a non-profit organization must obtain school permission five business days before they solicit their products on campus. This is a warning as we have confiscated several bags of candy and bootleg CD's. Owners of said products will be allowed to have their parents pick up their items on Saturdays only from 9am to 12pm.

"And finally, although we do not prohibit the wearing of certain colors, we do prohibit the wearing of gang paraphernalia. There following items are hereby banned on East Middle School property: head rags, baseball caps, checkered shirts in blue or red, tight shirts, revealing clothing, pants that do not fit around the waist, Timberlands or other forms of work boots. Also sports paraphernalia from the Colorado Rockies; the Chicago Bulls and any team who plays their home games in the State of California will no longer be allowed on campus.

"I reserve the right to add, subtract, multiply and divide from these rules at *any* time. Also every student will be given a list of rules that must be signed by Friday. Any student who does not bring back the form signed will be suspended until they do so. Your normal school day will resume under an abbreviated schedule."

The intercom went off and the police officer got up and stood before us. Our teacher had passed out a copy of the rules we were to sign. The police officer went into this speech about how he wanted our schools to be safe and how he didn't want to see no more kids get hurt and blasé blasé. I couldn't wait for him to stop so I could asked the question I had been dying to ask since I saw all these officers and stuff on school grounds. So when I got my opportunity, I spoke up.

"How come it took an elementary school student getting killed and a group of sixth graders who were fed up with living in a dictatorship to decide to overthrow the gangs before you guys decided to do anything about it?"

There were some oohs and aahs as people expected me to get in trouble for asking the question. The teacher and the police officer calmed everyone down so that they could answer the question.

"Sometimes, we as adults underestimate the pressures and problems that current students and children go through. When we were in school, we didn't have the gang problem and the violence that you guys are going through so we are not used to this either. We underestimated the gang problem at East Middle School and other schools in the area. It shouldn't have taken the death of a child or a group of rebellious students for us to decide to take action. Personally, had it been up to me, the gang members would have lost their rights to be students the minute they joined a gang. However, every gang member is not as vocal with their gang affiliation or going to school as students, so it is not easy to catch every gang member. Now, we have a task force dedicated to finding gang members and identifying them so that we can keep up with their illegal activities."

"So how long do you plan on staying here?" Lisa asked.

"As long as I am needed."

No one else had any questions and pretty soon, we went to our classes. We didn't get to socialize as often as we would have wanted to. For the most part, we just went to school, did some work and went to the next class. We went to our gym class and to my surprise Coach Spalding did not have any police officers with him or people escorting students to or from his class.

"Everyone have a seat!" Coach Spalding commanded as we entered the gymnasium. We did as we were told and once everyone was in class, he closed and locked the doors. I guess that meant that we weren't going outside, but again, I didn't expect to either. "On one hand, I admire you little sixth graders. It took a lot of guts for you to stand up to a local gang that could have killed you after the death of someone who was near and dear to you. I watched some of you do your thing and manhandle the gang members with pride and fear at the same time.

"On the other hand, although what you guys did was right in retrospect to your actions, you guys went about it the wrong way. You could have gotten yourselves and your fellow students killed. In some ways, you guys became the very thing you were fighting. Although I don't see you as a gang, many among the faculty do, and I understand where they are coming from, too.

"The principal and several teachers pushed for some of you to have the suspensions that the eighth graders are receiving. However, I and a few of my colleagues decided to speak up for you. We saw a distinct difference between what you were doing and what they were doing which is why you guys are still on campus. So I decided on the punishment that is going to be implemented for your actions. So I am going to give everyone one chance to own up to their role in this war. So if you were part of the war, not matter how big or how small of a role you played, I want y'all to stand up and jog around the gymnasium."

My eyes got big because with the doors closed, I came to realize the true size of the gymnasium. It was a lot bigger than I thought it would be. At first, no one got up and did anything. Coach Spalding made eye contact with me and several others in the room, letting us know that he knew we were part of it. "The alternative is to face expulsion."

One by one everyone got up in the room and ran laps around the gymnasium. I really didn't want to run because that seems like all I had been doing lately was running. But, this was better than getting suspended. Coach Spalding ran with us, which in some ways was cool except for the fact that some of us were tired of running. The running became jogging and the jogging turned into walking. When class was almost over, Coach Spalding released us so that we could shower and change clothes. It was times like this when I was glad that Mom made me bring an extra pair of underwear to put in my gym bag.

When school was over, students were escorted off campus by the police officers that had been there all day. Those of us that were walking to were told not walk near Elkhart so we had to take an alternate route. Lester was the only one allowed to go that way because his house was right there so he didn't get to hang out with us like that. Bernie, DeVante and Second walked home with us.

"Where's Allen?" Calvin asked.

"Allen got expelled with the rest of the gang members," Second replied.

I shook my head.

"I almost got expelled, too. I was in the principal's office for three hours man with 5-0 trying to determine whether or not I was a Blood. I know I'm not but I guess they wanted to be sure."

"I'm surprised they didn't catch y'all," Bernie said with a grin, "slick l'il bastards."

"Don't think we didn't get in trouble," Franklin replied, "we had essays to write with topics like, 'The Top Ten Reasons Gangs Are Bad for You' and 'I'm Too Young to Start a Revolution.'"

"They did not," DeVante thought we were lying.

"Yeah we did, too," Calvin complained, "my hand is hurting from all that writing I've been doing."

Calvin pretended like he was having problems balling his fist and we laughed at him. The rest of the walk we just cracked jokes on one another and reminisced on what was and dreamed about what was to become. We ran across 6th Avenue and we saw a police car put on his lights in the shopping center. He looked at us and pointed his finger and then drove off. I guess we can't do that no more either. When Calvin and I made it to his place, Carlton was kissing some chick near his door way. Calvin looked at me and kept walking to my crib.

"I swear that is not the girl he was kissing on this morning," Calvin said. I looked back and I could see them heading inside their apartment, "he's only doing this because he knows that our parents aren't coming in until later on tonight."

As we got closer to my apartment, we could see my father loading up the candy in the car. I guess it really was the end of the business and the dream, at least until I could think of something else. We put our stuff up and helped Dad put the rest of the candy that we were going to take back to the store.

"It's time for you to get a lawn mower," Dad told me.

"I don't want to cut lawns this summer," I protested.

"Well you need to figure out something if you expect to have your own business this summer."

I hadn't really thought about what kind of business I wanted to start. What would be good for the summer time anyway? I didn't want to mow lawns or walk around with my father selling hair products. I was still too young to work at Elitches. A car drove by playing music from the illegal rap station that had been operating off of the AM airwave. I saw this guy at the bus stop reading *The Source*, the hip-hop magazine that had been very hard to find in this area. On the way to the store, I saw people wearing hip-hop inspired clothing just like they were in the videos. I couldn't put my finger on what it was I wanted to do, but I knew that there was money in hip-hop since it was growing, I just had to figure out how I was going to get a piece of it.

When I don't catch any sleep...

Moesha and I had been kicking it for a little while. I didn't think I would like her when I first met her but as I got to know her she turned out real cool. When my boys found out that she and I were seeing each other, I got clowned. Calvin swore up and down that Moesha let him hit in the fourth grade but I know he was lying because Calvin's still scared of girls now. Ray and Trey were trying to feed me that nonsense about her messing with Second's older brother but I wasn't vibing to that. What would a high school sophomore want with a sixth grader?

Truth was, Moesha lived with her older aunt and cousin. Her mom died two years ago on a business trip to St. Louis and her father didn't want anything to do with her. Her cousin was about to graduate from Hinkley, so she didn't spend a lot of time with her. She seemed like the lonely type. We all met at Darren's house because he had a big ol' basement where his room was. The basement was set up like a miniature living room complete with a sofa; a small, round wooden table; a television and a few houseplants. Lester, Juan and Calvin were already there. Darren pulled out this domino table and he and Calvin were already playing and talking junk. I don't know who was winning 'cause neither one of them was keeping score. I sat at the table so I could watch and play whenever their game ended.

"I see Martin done come up to the table looking for a quick whooping," Calvin welcomed me to the table.

"Naw, naw, I don't go anywhere looking for no whooping. But I don't mind giving one anywhere though."

"Whatever man."

"You think you could whoop me?"

I looked at Calvin and smiled because we both knew the answer to that question.

"Don't get too into the game because the girls gonna be here any minute."

"Girls, what girls?" Juan asked.

"You should have told us the girls were going to be here 'cause I could have got some Trojans," Lester said.

"Negro please," Calvin shouted as he looked at him, "you ain't never hit none."

"Shut up punk! I've been hitting since I was ten," Lester responded.

"Grindin' your cousin doesn't count," Calvin got up from the table.

I shook my head because that was just nasty. I was more concerned for the fact that Lester didn't respond to or deny them actions…which was starting to make me look at him in a different light.

"Don't get too happy 'cause the only one getting some in this house is me," Darren watched Calvin and Juan anxiously put away the table, chairs, and stuff.

All this talk about sex was starting to make me think about it. I was trying to remember the last lie I told them about getting some so that when the question arises again, I could tell the same story. Truth was, I've never done it before. I wanted to and though I had come close a few times, but never actually did the deed. This girl did suck on it one time after I licked her breasts, but that doesn't count. I knew what they were doing, too. They're setting the room up so that we can play spin the bottle or truth or dare or some other mischievous game in the scheme of trying to get into the panties. I guess I was cool with it, I wasn't gonna leave and let everyone think I was a punk.

"Darren, I'm a run to the store real quick and get some Trojans," Juan said once everything was put away.

"I don't know why you are getting excited. Nobody is going to get none."

"Negro please, you know good and well that them girls are going to be down for whatever 'cause there are no parents around and besides, we might as well prepare for the main event...me getting laid."

"You can go if you want to but you not getting none. And we can put some money on that."

"Aight then, five dollars says that I will at *least* get some head before I go home."

"Oh let me get in on this," Lester pulled out a brand new five dollar bill.

"I'm a take my money in advance...thank you," Juan pulled out a five dollar bill.

"Let me go get my money real quick. Don't punk out when I come back," Darren said.

"Oh I won't," Juan promised.

I wasn't going to put no money on that because I have witnessed first hand Juan being able to con a girl out of some panties. In fact, he just got laid last week during lunch time in the boy's bathroom. I know this much because I walked in to pee and seen the girl and him coming out of the stall and him taking the condom off his piece.

"Come on Martin," Juan encouraged as he smiled and looked at me, "let's break bread together. You know I can do it."

"I know that you have the ability if the girl is willing, but I don't' have no money on me."

"Aight then, more for me."

Darren came back and he had a plastic bag and a paper, "this is a bet stating that Juan thinks he is going to get some head or some punany before the girls leave my house," Darren said as he was writing, "Calvin, Lester and Darren know this is not going to happen, but Juan thinks it is."

The guys looked at me one last time, but I still didn't have five dollars to put in the bag so I politely passed. After the guys put their money in the bag, Juan left the house to go to the store to get some Trojans. We sat down and watched some videos on BET.

"Man, we should have used that money to order us some pizza instead, what a waste," Lester complained as the Master P video came on.

"Look, if we win the bet, we can still get some pizza," Darren promised.

"True," Lester responded.

We watch a few other big booty girls shake it on the screen one last time and we turned the channel to see if Jerry Springer was on. Personally, I wanted to see the show just to see who was going to fight today. Yesterday, they had these two gay dudes going at it fighting over a girl. That's Jerry for ya. We finally found the channel that Jerry Springer was going to come on but we would have to wait thirty more minute. So we watched Montel Williams rip into someone about not paying their child support. By time the show was over with, Juan had come back with a twelve pack of Trojans. A few minutes later, the girls had rung the doorbell. Juan opened the box and gave each of us two condoms while he kept the rest for himself. We put the condoms in our pockets and we sat around watching Jerry Springer. Today's show was on "Wild and Horny Teenagers." How appropriate? Lisa, Angela, Pamela, Renee and Moesha walked down the stairs as they had some McDonald's bags in their hands.

"See, I told you these trifling niggas wasn't going to have no food," Lisa told Angela, "We should have made this a girls' only party."

"Naw, lets play with they minds," Pamela suggested, "The only reason they invited us is because they think we are going to give them some. See look at the numbers," Pamela continued as she pointed and counted to each of her girls the number of guys here.

"Naw, see you looking at this the wrong way," Juan said, "If there are five of you and five of us, no one can try anything. How come you didn't invite Dana?"

Dana was the girl who he got into the bathroom.

"Because, she handling some things. We know why you want to see Dana," Lisa responded.

"Yeah, we know why," Angela jumped in and the girls started laughing.

This was not looking good for Juan.

"You want to order some pizza?" Lester asked getting the money stash from under the table.

"Yeah, let's do that," Juan was quick to jump in.

"See, we weren't going to come over and not share. Each of us got you guys a meal since you were so gracious to play host," Lisa let everyone know.

Each of the girls sat next to a guy, pulled out a Quarter Pounder with Cheese, and split some fries. The guys said thank you and the girls welcomed us. I got my sandwich from Moesha and she smiled when she handed it to me.

"Ooh girl, Jerry Springer is on, turn this mug up!" Lisa yelled out excitedly.

We watched as Jerry Springer interviewed the parents and the horny teenagers, two of whom were trying to get it on onstage. Yeah, this is acting right here 'cause Jerry Springer would not get away with showing anything like that on television.

"So what do y'all want to do?" Lisa asked.

"Y'all the guest, what do y'all want to do?" Darren offered.

"Let's play truth or dare," Angela said boldly.

"But no freaky stuff," Pamela said, "I'm a good girl."

"Yeah she is," Lester said with a smile, which resulted in Pamela punching him in the chest.

"Who wants to go first?" Calvin asked.

"I'll go," Lisa said, "Darren, truth or dare?"

"Truth," Darren replied.

"Did y'all place a bet on who was going to get laid before we got here?" Lisa asked.

"Naw," Darren lied.

Good answer.

"You sure?" Lisa asked.

"I said no, girl!" Darren got a little agitated.

"Don't yell at me, I just asked you a simple question," Lisa said.

"My turn," Darren scanned the room, "Angela, truth or dare."

"Dare," Angela said boldly, looking dead at Darren as she dared him to ask her to do something stupid.

"Aight, I dare you to kiss the floor."

"Aw hell naw," Angela yelled, "ain't no telling what you done did to this floor."

"Let's play something else," Darren suggested, "I knew the minute I asked a question one of you would punk out."

Angela kissed the floor and wiped her lips off afterwards, "aight, *Darren* truth or dare?"

"Truth"

"See, I knew you was going to do that, that is why my question is a truth and a dare. How big is your thing? And don't lie 'cause I might need to take a ruler to get some proof."

"I got you. Seven. And it's big enough for you." Darren asked.

"Whatever," Angela said as her and Pamela slapped hands and smiled.

"Aight Moesha, truth or dare?"

"Truth," Moesha replied in an assertive yet sexy voice.

"Are you a virgin?"

"Oh hold up!" Lisa jumped up in the air, "What kind of game is this?"

"I asked if Moesha is a virgin. Angela took it to that level when she asked how big my thing was so I should be able to ask whether or not Moesha is a virgin." Darren defended his question.

"Naw, Lisa it's cool. I can answer the question. No, Darren, I'm not a virgin. But I'm not loose either." Moesha answered to the amazement of her home girls.

"Thank you Moesha."

"Juan, truth or dare," Moesha asked.

"Dare," Juan responded, up for the challenge.

"I dare you to close your eyes and let me do whatever I want to do to you," Moesha said.

"I'm cool with that," Juan closed his eyes.

Moesha sat there and we watch her to see what she was going to do, then she said, "I'm done."

"What did you do?" Juan moved around to make sure nothing was on him or anything.

"I didn't do anything," Moesha laughed and the rest of the room started laughing.

"Aight, Lisa truth or dare," Juan said.

"Dare, fool! I ain't scared," Lisa said like she was soldier.

"I want you to humble yourself and kiss my feet," Juan said.

All of us couldn't help but laugh. I never thought in a million years that Lisa could be humble to anybody. But she got on her knees, kissed Juan's feet and she snuck a punch in to his stomach.

"That's what you get," Lisa said as her friends started laughing, "Trying to make me kiss your nasty feet. What kind of woman do you think I am? But you know what? I'm not even going to mess with you any more. I'm a get on Lester for laughing the loudest. Nigga, truth or dare? And you better say dare!"

"Truth!" Lester shouted loudly.

"I would have said truth, too," Calvin said.

"Oh you are a punk. Okay, answer this, why you walk like a little girl? Got that nice butt of yours shaking, shake better than me." Lisa asked and her friends started laughing again.

"Forget you Lisa!" Lester said.

"No sweetie, it's forget you."

"I got this," Lester said a little angry, "Moesha truth or dare."

"Truth," Moesha responded.

"Lisa's a B sometimes right," Lester looked dead at her, "I mean you can say it. You are answering my question."

"We *all* can be B's sometimes, ain't that right girls."

"That's right," all of them chimed in like a choir.

"Aight, who hasn't been picked yet...Martin, truth or dare?" Moesha asked me.

"Dare," I looked her dead in the eyes.

"I dare you to get butt naked and let us see everything." Moesha said with a grin.

"Oh gosh!" Calvin cried above the sound of some uughs from the guys.

I stood up. I was proud of my shape. I wasn't the best looking brotha in the world but I could at least walk outside with my shirt off and catch a few stares. At least that was what I wanted to think. I took my shoes off first, then my socks. Then I took off my shirt and put it on the floor. I dropped my pants and my draws in one motion and I stepped out. Then I did a nice little turn so the girls could see all of me. I saw smiles on each of their faces. I started to put my clothes on but I changed my mind, I put a shirt over my stuff and sat on my draws, which were still on the floor.

"Aight, Moesha, I hope you liked what you saw." I said to her.

"I did," she answered.

"Yeah, you was alright," Lisa said. The guys opened their eyes.

"Why you still naked?" Calvin asked.

"This is part of my dare. Moesha you accept?" I said.

"Yeah," she replied.

"I dare you to give me some."

I don't even know what made me say it. I didn't even think the words could come out of my mouth. I was so nervous that I got hard, anticipating Moesha answering my dare with some real punany. I could feel the sweat starting to from across my forehead, lining up like soldiers getting ready to go to war.

"Oh hell no! This..." Lisa snatched the shirt from my thighs and exposing my erection, "you ain't got to do this Moesha. His little as...oh!" Lisa looked at me, "You ain't... ain't...ain't...aw, lets go."

The guys put their hands over their eyes again, disgusted with me while the girls just looked at me in awe. I didn't understand why, it's not like I was showing myself. I looked around the room, I realized how stupid I was for even saying something like that, and I started to put my clothes on. I had changed my mind about the whole thing and walked away. Well, I was until Moesha grabbed my hand and pulled me next to her.

***

The walk home from Darren's house seemed longer than I thought it should be. I felt a little heavier, probably from the dampness of the actions that had just taken place. I have no regrets. I'm happy that I *finally* got to do what I had been lying to everyone about doing for the past two years. But now what? It was good, but it wasn't all that. I didn't feel any firecrackers or any bright lights go off around me. I felt good, don't get me wrong but the only thing that's changed about me now is that I stink. I can wash that off but I can't wash away what I can't get back.

I stepped into the house and I didn't even notice Marcus, Ray, Trey and my father sitting in the living room.

"Sup Martin," Ray hugged me. I replied but I felt funny 'cause as his body pressed against mine, I could feel the wetness on me. Ray stepped back and looked at me, but he did not say anything. "You might want to zip your fly," Ray pointed out to me.

I looked down to zip my fly and when I looked up and I didn't feel that my father was standing over me. I looked up and he damn near scared the hell out of me. He touched my neck, which felt a little soft thanks to Moesha.

"What's that smell man, you been getting some?" Dad asked me.

"Let me take a shower," I tried to make it to the bathroom but instead he put his hand on my hickie and squeezed it and flung me on the chair.

"Naw, nigga, you going to tell me about this girl you done gave your virginity to," my father was a little upset, "did you hit it from the back?"

I looked at him 'cause I could not believe he had the gall to ask me that. I looked at Ray and Trey and hoping that they might bail me out.

"I think it's time for us to go," Trey got up and heading toward the door.

"Yeah," Ray looked at me again, "I'll talk to y'all later."

Man!

"So tell me little Negro, you think you grown? Were you getting some?"

"Yeah, Dad, I was getting some," I responded like a little punk. I could have punched myself in the jaw for that remark.

"Oh, so you lied to me about going to Darren's house?"

"No."

"So did you go before or after you got you some? I hope you went before 'cause you should know you stink!"

I've never heard my father say the N-word in that reference until now. Man, I don't know what to think; my father using words like *getting some*, and *hitting it from the back*. I hope he don't talk about my mom like that.

"Was it good? How many did you bust or wait, did you bust one?" my father continued, his questioning was starting to make me hate him.

"Why you asking me questions? You already know." I responded. Bad choice.

"Oh I know! I know that I told my son that he could go over Darren's house and hang out for a little while 'cause you didn't have no homework. I didn't tell you to go off and have sex with some chick."

At this point I looked away from him 'cause I was so tempted to punch him in his damn grill for invading *my* privacy like that. He got in my face. He slapped my head. I had grit on my face then 'cause I was beginning to wish that I were still a virgin. I didn't understand what the big deal was. My father stepped back and as he did, the door was unlocked and I could see my mother walk in. "On second thought, I don't want you to answer that question. I want you to get out of my face and take a bath!"

I grabbed a clean pair of clothes and I rushed to the shower. I locked the door so my father's crazy self wouldn't try to come in there and whoop me. I cleaned myself and tried to hear whether or not he was yelling or still mad but all I could hear was the water hitting the walls. When I was done, I put on my clothes and ran to my room.

Dad was not as mad as he was the first time I walked in the door. He started rubbing his hand over his face as he sat down on the bed next to me.

"I'm disappointed in you," my father started off, "I'm mad because you probably didn't put no thought into the actions that you got yourself into. You didn't ask this chick if she had AIDS, gonorrhea, syphilis or none of that. I know you didn't 'cause I wouldn't have either.

"I was hoping that you would have saved yourself until you got married. I know we had the sex talk and everything. We talked about what you should and should not do, but don't you remember anything I said about *marriage*. I was blessed that I had a level head 'cause my virginity was the best gift I could have given your mother, and hers was the best gift she could have given me. I was hoping that you would have figured out without me telling you that we made you on our wedding night."

I hate when my father talked to me like that 'cause he has a way of making me feel like crap.

"You brought your little hard-headed self out here a little early, but that was our union man. Look, I can't tell you what you can and can't do, you are going to do what you want to do anyway. I'm not going to ground you. I want you to think about what you did and what you might do in the future. And at this point, I'm going to let it go."

I was happy when my father got up and left, but I was sad at the fact that I don't think that I measured up to my father's expectations. The phone rang and Marcus came into the room to let me know that it was for me. I went the living room and answered the phone and my mom looked at me. I couldn't tell if she was disappointed or not, but she left the room.

"Martin," I could hear Moesha on the other end.

"Sup Moesha."

"I don't want you to think that I do that on the regular. You the second guy that I messed around with and I only do that for my boyfriends."

Dad lied…Moesha did think I was special cause I'm her boyfriend and she gave it up to me. "I understand. I didn't mean to put you in a position like that." I apologized anyway because in hindsight, I shouldn't have put her on the spot like that.

"Naw, I did that to you when I dared you to take your clothes off. I thought about you."

I smiled, "you did?"

"Before and after, but I didn't think I was going to get with you like that."

"Oh." I was slightly disappointed.

"So where does this leave us?"

"Friends I hope. I gave you something." I was excited, like I was getting ready to share a big secret with her.

"What did you give me?"

"My virginity," I gulped.

"Oh…I guess we got to be friends then. Look, let me talk to you tomorrow alright."

"Alright, it was nice hearing from you."

"Nice hearing from you, too."

I heard the phone line disconnect and I put the phone on the receiver. I thought about her response to the fact that I gave my virginity to her and how she blew it off. I guess my father was right, I was so happy to be doing something that I didn't even think about what I was doing. And I can't get *that* back.

Because He has come at last, and I didn't miss a peep...

Peace. That was what I have been waiting for this whole year. Now that I got it, I don't know what to do with it. My brother and I have Spring Break this week and I am playing catch with him. Lester was playing catch with him, too. I thought my boy was better, but honestly, I don't think he will be the same. He doesn't look as sad as he was, but he was not the happy go lucky boy we used to know either. He's also lost some weight, too. He says it's from eating healthy and exercising, but I know some of that was from being sad and depressed. I worry about him sometimes, but as long has he's okay then that's all that matters. Cisco and Arnez also show up and pretty soon, we all were playing catch with my little brother. Carlton, Calvin, and Casey come outside once they see and hear all of us playing. Pretty soon, we're not playing catch but just hanging out and enjoying the first day of spring. Someone had "Summertime" by DJ Jazzy Jeff & the Fresh Prince blasting from their stereo. With the wind chill it clearly isn't "summer time" but we'll take it for what it is.

In no time, a pretty young thing walks through the park and Carlton was off chasing her. The fellas were laughing at him because the woman wasn't giving him any play. It was good to have that fool back to his normal self. Moesha, Angela, Lisa and Pamela showed up a little later. I walked up to Moesha, hoping that we could talk. She hasn't returned any of my calls since we were together. I guess you could say I was whipped, okay, maybe a little horny too because I did want another stab at it, but I just wanted to hang with her again. I wasn't the "hit it then quit it" type of brother.

"You keep calling me," Moesha started off frustrated.

"You keep ignoring me," I responded. "Why don't you call me back?"

"You must be dumber than dumb! I don't want to be with you anymore. I got me a new man."

"A new…you know what, that's cool. If that's how you want to play things."

I left her and everyone else at the park. I started to get Marcus but I didn't feel like being bothered. Plus, he was having fun so I had to let him go. I felt stupid thinking Moesha and I had something. Truth was, the writing was on the wall about what kind of girl she was. Everyone knew and could see it but me. And that's okay. What's the song called, "Everybody Plays the Fool?" I guess I was *Boo-boo the fool* today but I won't be tomorrow.

"Why you look like you got your lip stuck out?" I didn't know I had walked all the way to Allen's crib. Didn't even know he stayed in the same apartment complex. The cannabis was roasting in the air and I watched blunts get passed from Allen to Second to Allen's crew.

"I got problems,"

"I can see that. I was asking why the lip was stuck out? You look like some chick just broke your heart."

I walked away because I didn't need Allen or them other cats in my business. I could feel Allen following me and the smell of cannabis getting stronger. My nose felt a little wider as I inhaled the second hand smoke.

"Look man, you can't be giving these little girls your heart and stuff. You got to hit it and quit it. Get your main girl, get one on the side to mess around with and go on about your business."

I looked at him. I knew he was telling me he was cheating on Shanice and if I were still love struck over her that would be a problem but I'm not so it ain't.

"You ever smoke weed before?" Allen asked as he slowly blew the smoke from his mouth.

"No."

"You should. It'll relax your mind and make you forget about her at the same time."

I had to admit the smell was getting to me. I always liked the way the herb lingered in the air and I seemed to benefit from the natural high without having to inhale. A part of me wanted to try it—be a big boy for once. But I knew that Dad preached against it and Mom would flip if she even thought I'd let someone who smoked get too close to me.

"I can't smoke, I got asthma," I told a half-lie, my brother had asthma and at that moment, I felt around for his inhaler. I didn't have it and I was hoping he had it on him. I needed to continue this lie so that the temptation wouldn't overtake me.

"Man, don't be such a punk. Go ahead and take a puff. Come back over with my boys so we don't get in trouble."

I needed to be a punk—I couldn't inhale. "I'm good."

"I hate when people tell me no. 'Specially if I'm trying to help them out!"

"I didn't say no, I said I'm good because I can't." I smirked.

"Me and your l'il cocky ass is gonna fight one of these days." Allen shook his head and grinned. He inhaled again and then blew another hard smoke my way. If I didn't know better, I'd think he was toying with me. I shook my head at him and laughed. Luckily for me, he was laughing, too.

"Raise up fool!" I heard someone yell and I remembered my little brother in the park and ran in that direction. Allen, Second and his boys were following me. I quickly ran over to where I last seen Marcus and I couldn't find him. I moved toward the crowd and started searching for Marcus. I saw Lisa moving him behind her and I went in that direction. In the center of the crowd, Garfield and Carlton looked as if they were going to go at it again, "if I had known where you lived I would have come by to finish off you and your brother."

Carlton didn't waste any time, delivering two quick blows to Garfield's dome, reminding him of the ass whooping he gave Garfield a few weeks ago. Garfield ducked back and Carlton followed with two more punches and a quick trip move that I saw in Mortal Kombat. Garfield fell on his back and Carlton followed throwing more blows to his face. While watching Carlton whoop on Garfield again, I could see Second and Allen and his crew manhandling Tony, Cedric and some other guys in Garfield's crew. What happened to peace? I quickly grabbed Marcus and Casey, pulling them away from Carlton and Garfield and walked away from the war zone. Lisa and Pamela came after me and they each grabbed a boy by the hand.

"You need to get back in there and handle that!" Lisa said with seriousness on her face. She smiled and quickly kissed me on the cheek, "we'll look after the boys."

I ran to the war zone and helped Second with one of the bigger boys he was tackling. Second seemed happy that I was helping him. To be short man, he's got a lot of heart and I guess that was one of the reasons I hung out with him like that to begin with. We kept throwing punches until we heard a gun go off. My instinct was to run but something told me to turn around. I did to see Calvin holding the gun to Garfield's face.

I heard Allen yell an explicative as he was feeling around for his piece. "Calvin, tell me that's not my piece?"

"Don't worry, you'll get it back. I'm just gonna do this real quick." Calvin promised as he closed the gap between him and Garfield.

"I don't have no bodies on that one man, you need to give that back."

"Shut up!" Calvin yelled at Allen as he hit Garfield with it.

"Calvin, give me the gun," Carlton tried to reason with Calvin, "I done already whooped his butt twice already. He ain't gonna mess with us no more."

"Naw," Calvin shook his head and steadily aim the gun at Garfield's face again, "I'm a kill this fool just like he killed Carla. And then I'm get at his boys."

"Don't kill this fool in broad daylight man," Allen tried to reason with him. "Look at all these witnesses you got out here. You'll go to prison with the grown folks and you'll never get out."

Calvin wasn't trying to hear that. I looked at Garfield's crew and was surprised to know that despite the fact of being armed, they didn't pull out their pieces. I thought that was unusual that they were just going to let Calvin put a gun to Garfield's face like that. Most Crips I knew would have been took the chance and took a shot at Calvin by now.

"I don't care if I go to prison. I care about avenging my sister's death. Only thing I hate is that Cola's butt ain't out here so that I could finish her off, too."

"Yo, Cal, just because Garfield is a Crip doesn't mean that he killed Carla." Allen tried to reason with him again.

"He did!" Garfield looked at me and between the two of us we knew he was telling the truth. "I always knew this sucka was behind Carla's death. Ever since she's been gone I could feel it every time I see this cat. I don't feel it around Tony or Cedric or them other Crips. I feel it with him and I don't like it. But as soon as I pull this trigger, I won't feel it no more. And don't think I haven't forgotten about Sammie either!"

Garfield looked down. We all knew about Sammie because with the exception of Second, Allen and his crew, we all were there when that happened. Garfield sat and just looked at Calvin.

"Cola was never Carla's friend. I was just using that dumb broad to get at Carla so I could get at her man. Don't act like you didn't know who Carla's man was and don't act like she wasn't a Blood because she was," Garfield tried to defend himself but Calvin wasn't trying to hear that. In his mind, all he needed to know was that Garfield killed Carla.

"Carla wasn't no Blood," Allen said. "Carla didn't even like us like that. She loved De'Angelo for the man he was and he loved her for the woman she was. They fought all the time because he wanted her to be down with the set, but she just wasn't down like that. The only person you ever seen Carla roll with like that was Cola and that was because she really looked at Cola like a sister. We tried to tell her about Cola and Cola being a Crip and all of that, but she wasn't trying to hear us. Between being worried about if she was going to Spelman and being with her man, she couldn't see Cola for what she really was, a trifling, snake trick! Carla had hopes of getting out of here and marrying her man because she really thought she could get him out of the game and change him. If Carla was wrong for anything, she was wrong for believing that."

"Whatever man, you just covering for her. But you know what, I killed that trick because she was with the wrong man, at the wrong place and at the wrong time and as soon as I get up, I'm going to kill this punk and his brother, too!"

"Reach for yours then!" I knew then if I hadn't known it before that Calvin had lost his damn mind. How you gonna let another cat reach for his piece? Everyone ran away from Calvin and Garfield trying to get to the side hoping not to get caught by a stray. Garfield backed away and stood up and quickly drew for his. He pulled it out and shot a shot and Calvin shot a shot. Garfield was falling down and Calvin shot another shot at his heart. This time, the bullet was faster and just ripped through Garfield chest and came out coated with crimson blood. Calvin aimed at Garfield's face and just before he landed on the ground, a bullet landed in his head. "I told you I was quick."

Calvin threw the gun down on the ground next to Garfield, which I thought was crazier. When I looked around, I didn't see Tony, Cedric or anyone else in Garfield's crew. I guess they weren't with him like that to begin with, "you can have your gun back."

Allen waved his hand and acted like he was pushing it away, "It's yours now. I don't want it."

Carlton walked up and just as we could hear the police sirens, he picked up the gun and shot another shot at Garfield's body. Carlton rubbed his bare hand on the gun and held the gun down toward his side.

"What are you doing?" Allen yelled.

"If anyone asked, I did this," Carlton cried. I knew what he was doing and to tell the truth, I could say that I would have done the same, "you guys hear me, *I* did this!" The way he pointed at his chest made it seem like he was proud of himself. I guess in some ways, he had a right to be.

The police came through the crowd and they ordered Carlton to put the gun down and to lie on the ground. Carlton did as he was told and the police rushed in, handcuffed him and picked him.

"Not going to miss this one," one of them said looking at Garfield's body. He shook his head and looked at Carlton, "I don't even know this one."

They took Carlton away and he stopped and looked at me, "watch after my brother man. Make sure he stays out of trouble. Do that for me and I'll owe you."

The police laid a white sheet over Garfield's body and marked the grass. Another set of plain clothes police officers took pictures and picked up gun shells and collected evidence. Casey was crying and I took him and Marcus from the girls. Calvin sat on the curb and was crying. Calvin looked up and Carlton grinned at him.

"Stay out of trouble man, I got this. That's all you got to do."

They put Carlton in the police car and they drove off. Calvin was still crying as he reached for Casey and he held him tight. He shot his way into a new responsibility, that of being the bigger brother. We walked into my apartment as my dad was just getting in.

"I need to call my mom Mr. Little," Calvin held Casey tight, who was still crying on his shoulder.

"What's going on outside? Where's Carlton?" my father asked.

"He's not coming back."

My dad seen the blood on Calvin's shirt as he put Casey down and he motioned for me to follow him into my room. Dad closed the door so that Calvin could talk on the phone in private. Marcus was looking out the window.

"Why does Calvin have blood all over his shirt?"

"Because Carlton found who killed Carla."

My dad looked at me and he knew that I knew that he knew I was lying. He didn't question me though, but I knew that we would have this conversation at a later date. When Calvin was finished he came into the room. We sat on the bed and I watched Calvin cry on my father's shoulder. My father held his head and rocked him as if he were his own son. Calvin got what he wanted, but he didn't think about the consequences of his actions. In killing Garfield, he may have avenged his sister's death, but it cost him his brother's life. I could tell by the look in his eyes that he felt worse now than he did before he pulled the trigger. That's when I realized that every life had a cost and if you are going to take one, you need to be willing to pay for it. Through the tears, I could see that Calvin was in agony and when he cried he let out a deep, guttural moan! The time for payment had arrived.

Before your leave,
check out the next *worth fighting 4* joint,

Nothing Is 4 Nothing

Available wherever books are sold

Chapter One
Lester

I smiled when I saw Martin and Franklin walking onto the basketball court at our old elementary school. With days before school was set to start, the playground was surprisingly busy. A football team was practicing for an upcoming game, with a cheer squad doing tumbles and pyramids. I checked the court. It wasn't like the other guys to be late.

"Sup homes." Martin greeted me and brought me in for a hug.

I felt a little strange. I avoided hugs since Sammie's been gone, but I didn't leave him hanging. The excitement of us getting back together to hustle and make money for the new school year had me hooked. When we were selling candy last year, I easily brought home almost $200 a week selling premade drink mixes, large jawbreakers, Airheads, Now-N-Laters and other candies typically only sold in candy stores. I didn't have any more money. I gave most of it to help my parents bury my brother. They put the rest in a kid savings account I added my allowance to monthly.

"What's up!" I could hear Calvin imitating Martin Lawrence by saying the catchphrase three times. I was hoping he wouldn't spoil the show. I can only watch *Martin, Living Single* and *New York Undercover* on the weekends after my mom and Mr. Stewart, Sammie's white Jamaican daddy, watched the shows first.

I was surprised to see Calvin out of the house. Ever since he pulled the trigger and got rid of the bully, his parents have kept him locked up like he was on lockdown in a prison. For most of the summer, we only saw him through the window, and on those rare occasions we caught him going to and coming from his therapist. I always wanted to find out what it would be like to talk to a therapist. If it would be worth me going for myself. I had some things I wanted to talk about, but now wasn't the time.

Darren and another boy who came up to his shoulders were headed in our direction. Darren didn't get taller, but he was starting to look a little more like a power forward for a college basketball team. As they got closer, I couldn't believe the guy walking next to him was Juan. It seemed like the last time I saw him, he was a little runt. He barely stood as high as my shoulders. Now Juan was easily a few inches taller than my five foot six frame.

The smile fell from Martin's face as Darren and Juan began gripping everybody. Something wasn't right. Martin was always a jovial spirit. He always wanted to see everyone happy. Martin would do anything to not only get the money, but help ensure his friends got paid, too.

Martin started to choke to get everybody's attention. I knew something was up with him, but like I said, I didn't wanna call him out on it right now. I knew eventually Martin would tell me what's going on and which of my two boys have pissed him off.

"I know it's been a minute since we've all been together running the halls of East Middle School."

The group of us got excited. I got a good look at Martin, and realized he was changing, too. Seemed like all of us in our group were going through our phases. Martin didn't get taller, but I did notice his voice got a little deeper. He also grew out his hair. I was surprised his parents let him rock corn rolls. Then again, his dad still sold hair products for M.Walker Products. It was no telling what product his dad was pumping in his hair.

"We go back to school in two weeks," Franklin pointed out, "I'm ready to see these girls. And just kick it." We all looked at Franklin like he was crazy. For one, we wondered what lie he told his aunt to get her to agree to walk with Martin up to the school. Two, Franklin was scared of girls. I graduated to giving them full on hugs and sneaking a pat on their booties. Franklin hugged these chicks from the side. He wouldn't hold their hands when offered. He always asked one of us to come with him whenever he had to talk to one. I knew he wasn't into dudes cause he swore he wanna be down with Brandy. I also knew his auntie watched him like a hawk. I get it. She's the only family he has left and he doesn't want to disappoint her or end up in the system where he could never see us again. I say live a little. I bet he thought they still had cooties.

"I didn't come here to think about no girls." Calvin articulated in a tone that made all of us hush. "I came here to find out about how we was gonna make some money. And I know my boy Martin got a plan."

"Yeah, I do." Martin confidently stepped closer to the center. The sun was working overtime to roast us on the court. The shine on his forehead made him look like one of those milk dud candies. "My parents agreed to let me set up shop with the candy store again. They said no guns, no gangs, no fighting."

"We don't have to worry about none of that because Garfield's gone, and we haven't seen Freddie, Tony or Cedric's punk asses." Juan grew excited.

I caught the way Martin rolled his eyes at Juan. I glanced at Calvin and knew he caught it, too. I had no idea what happened between Martin and Juan over the summer, but whatever it was had me a little concerned.

"I just don't want Sammie's death to be in vain." I hated bringing up the past. I still hadn't healed from it.

"How are you holding up?" Juan asked.

"Taking it day by day. Praying the nightmares away." That part was true. My mom and Mr. Stewart kept me active in a church my mom was familiar with. I have moments where I felt like I failed him as an older brother. I didn't protect him or save his life. It should have been me that caught that bullet, not him.

"You're not the only one, I've been having them, too." Calvin admitted. "Even with me seeing a therapist the thoughts in my head never go away."

I wouldn't dare trade his weight for mine. I heard stories about how young men who became murderers eventually turn into monsters. I hope I always stayed on Calvin's good side or that he never thought to turn a gun on either of us. I had so many questions I wanted to ask Calvin. I wanted to know how Carlton was holding up since he took the rap for him? How was he with Casey? I wished I had a little brother to bug me to death. One that wanted to be up under me all the time. That's been the hardest part about losing Sammie, realizing I didn't appreciate the time I had with him.

"Are you looking to add candy or do something different this year?" Darren asked. "We gotta do something to keep them interested in buying from us again."

The smile on Martin's face returned. I knew he had something up his sleeve.

"I want to see if we can find something hot that we can get our hands on before it hits the stores, but if it ain't broke, I'm not trying to fix it." Martin stated. "I was actually looking at selling mix tapes."

"What?!" All of us were collectively confused. What were we doing with some mixtapes?

"Hear me out—we already got a customer base with the candy. A lot of us have the same taste in music, too. There's two ways we can do this. One, we can catch when Best Buy and Circuit City drop the tapes at $6.99. Buy only the stuff we know is going to be popping then sell them at $9.00, which will be less than the $10.99 they hike the price up to after the first week release."

Martin was about to piss me off. I sling candy, not tapes. "Safe plan," I said. "But it ain't making us the kind of money we used to. It's more upfront money. Another option is we can buy a large group of tapes and CDs from independent record labels. Build our own mobile record store. I know one of the guys that works for No Limit Records."

The rest of us looked at Martin like he was crazy.

"No Limit Records," Juan questioned, "who's that?"

"Master P and them." Martin was excited. I knew he was knee deep into this idea. One thing I respected about Martin was if he wanted us to jump in something, he's tried the idea out first or at least he's talked with his parents about it before pitching it to us. I loved the hustler in him but my God, every idea ain't meant to be jumped on. "Look, I know Master P isn't well known now but one day, he's gonna be big and you're gonna wanna have the jump on this."

Martin pulled out copies of two albums, *Mama's Bad Boy* and *The Ghetto's Trying to Kill Me!* The way our eyes almost popped out of our sockets. *The Ghetto's Trying to Kill Me!* had a pic of a young lady laying on top of Master P giving him the business. I saw the fear in Franklin's eyes–ain't no way in hell he jumping in on this.

"YO!!!" I shouted. "Your moms is never gonna let this fly."

"And how did you get this past your daddy?" Juan questioned.

"Yeah man," Calvin tore into the cassette trying to see if he could see more action in the album liner. "Ain't no way any of our parents are going to let us get away with this."

"Where are we gonna hide these?" Darren asked.

"That's the best part–they got to order the tape from us." Martin really thought this through. "We aren't carrying copies of this tape. They got to order it from us and then I'll deliver it or have it sent from my cousin's recording studio. He built one in his basement and he sells a lot of independent rap artists from the west coast and the south. We have access to other rappers, too."

"You done lost yo' rabid ass mind." Juan looked Martin up and down and smacked his teeth.

"I'm gonna make you lose yours in a minute." Martin stepped forward, dropped his bag and balled his fist.

I knew it! Calvin, Darren, Franklin and I quickly jumped in to separate these two. We already won the war against Garfield–we didn't need to be fighting against each other.

"What the hell is wrong wit' y'all?" I was surprised to hear Franklin lose his cool. He was usually more even tempered than Martin.

"He just mad I put my bone in Moesha." Juan smirked.

I shook my head and continued to push Juan back while keeping my eye on Franklin. Martin used to "date Moesha", if you can call it that. Before everything went down, Martin fell head over heels over this girl everyone had a piece of. Martin gave this girl his virginity and then got salty when she dumped him saying "she wanted to be friends." Martin had feelings for the girl and Juan was violating. I can't even co-sign that. I also knew Martin went against the advice Calvin and I gave him and he's still putting his stick into the girl. Ugh! No lie, I saw it with my own eyes—more than once. Every time Moesha isn't talking to some dude and trying to compare who got the bigger piece, he up in there. And he don't wear condoms all the time. I have no idea what She's doing to this boy, but she got him a chokehold and he can't let go.

"Juan, you wrong," Calvin put it out there.

"How?!?!" Juan broke away from me. I was worried. I didn't want him to take a step closer to Martin. I didn't want to see my boys fight. "I'm not the only one putting stick in her."

Shut up! BRO! That only made Martin try to rush him. They started cussing at each other and threatening to whoop each other's asses. Boy, this wasn't the way this was supposed to go at all.

"Yo! Chill before the adults get here and we get kicked out." Franklin warned as he looked around.

"Man, forget this!" Juan started walking away. "I don't need him to make money. I'm out!"

Martin grabbed his bag and headed the opposite way down Elkhart Street toward 6th Avenue. "I'mma put this on ice and come back."

Franklin rushed to catch up with him and I knew he was trying to calm him down.

"Let me make sure Juan cools off and them two fools don't try to meet up no where." Darren exhaled as he gripped us and gave chase after Juan.

"Aight man, later." I was a little pissed. I was ready to get our money up and these two are about to let some chicken head get in the way of our bread.

"These jokers," Calvin shook his head and chuckled. "Juan should have kept his mouth shut."

I looked at Calvin sideways. *"You knew?!"*

"Don't play dumb, man," Calvin started walking toward the apartment complex he and Martin stayed in. Calvin reached in his pocket and pulled out a box of menthol cigarettes. Before I could ask, he lit one up. I'm learning more new things about my boys every day. "A part of the reason I came out was because I'd have enough time to sneak and smoke this before I got home. Can't have Casey telling on me.

"Anyway, Moesha does the nasty every day and twice on Sundays." Calvin took a strong drag from the cigarette. He offered me a puff but I turned it down. "She'll hop off of Martin at the top of one hour and be on top of Juan by time the next hour come. I see everything from the window. Martin acting like he don't know what's going? That's crazy. I told them Juggernauts *'stop banging Moesha! Everyone banging Moesha! There's got to be another girl besides Moesha!'* They do what they wanna do, man."

I heard sex was a powerful drug—and I was watching it in real time. By the time we walked two more blocks, the cigarette was gone. Once we hit 6th Avenue a few minutes later, there was almost no trace of the cigarette I know Calvin smoked. He had it down to a science.

"You not worried about Martin and Juan?" I couldn't believe Calvin was so cool, calm and collected about this.

"Hell no–if them little kids weren't around, I'd woulda said let them fight. They need to get that out just like Arnez and I had to get ours out. Watch, I bet good money after they squabble, we're gonna hear about how she had both of them at the same time."

I chuckled cause I could almost picture it. "You stupid."

We both looked across the street. Running across 6th Avenue was just as dangerous as driving on I-70 or 225. We did our best Quincy Watts impression and made it across the street safely. We checked to make sure we was good– something each of us did out of habit. We've experienced having friends and loved ones get hit by cars.

"I'm serious. Let Martin and Juan get it off and we'll be good. Besides, iron sharpens iron." Calvin barely caught his breath.

I shook my head. Leave it to him to twist the Bible. "That's not what the verse means."

Calvin flashed his pearly whites. "I know." We walked past the Albertsons and were on the apartment complex property. "If we hurry up, we can catch Martin before he gets to his apartment."

That was Calvin's way of asking to race. "You know I can't run fast."

"We done already got so much of that fat off of you." Calvin bragged. Bastard. "Time to get the rest."

Can't get mad cause Calvin has been part of my weight loss journey. Last year, I was a chunky ass dude–got called Fat Albert and Webster all the time. Now, I look like a respectable defensive end. I looked at Calvin and I put my foot to the pavement. Didn't matter if I beat him. I just knew I had to keep going.

Up next,

Boyz 4 Life

Franklin has always bragged about how Winston-Salem, North Carolina was his dream home and wants nothing more than to leave the thuggish, ruggish gangster ways of Denver behind. Upon arriving, he finds that the city was not the one he visited in the summertimes. He can't get a long with anyone except for Mike, a fourteen year old bad ass who happens to be gay. As Franklin and Mike grow up, they find that friendship is important and help each face obstacles. When something happens to potentially end one of their lives, will these young men be able to face this challenge together?

Available wherever books are sold

ABOUT THE AUTHOR

Over the years, Isaiah David Paul has written in a variety of genres and became a writing partner and ghostwriter for a few award-winning and best-selling authors. With his string of successes and renewed faith in God, Isaiah David Paul has finally decided to follow his calling to write under his own name. He has a business management degree from North Carolina Agricultural & Technical State University, a Masters of Entrepreneurship from Western Carolina University and a MAT-Elementary Education from the University of North Carolina at Greensboro. He is the author of over fifty titles under various pseudonyms and has contributed to the publication of nearly two hundred books. He lives a private life with his family in the Southeast United States

Visit Me Online at www.IsaiahDavidPaul.com

Follow Me on Twitter: @isaiahdavidpaul
Follow Me on Instagram: @isaiahdavidpaul

Like My Facebook Page: Isaiah David Paul

Email Me: isaiahdavidpaul@gmail.com